GIRL WITH THE GUN

SYDNEY RYE MYSTERIES
BOOK 8

EMILY KIMELMAN

Heading illustration: Autumn Whitehurst
Cover Design: Christian Bentulan
Formatting: Jamie Davis

CHAPTER ONE

Suds slipped down my body and gathered at my ankles before traveling in a flotilla to the drain. The white, iridescent bubbles jiggled as droplets of water crashed around them. They popped one by one, the mass sinking into the pipe as each individual bubble lost tension and let go.

Letting go is an art.

And I am not an artist.

I'm a killer.

It's not for pleasure, though there is some of that. Lady Justice is tantamount to my god. I serve her single-mindedly, but there is no blindfold. I am prejudice, human—so human.

Would the world be safer with me under lock and key? One less terrorist wreaking havoc. Or more dangerous? One less soldier fighting for justice.

Blue barked. I looked through the fogged glass seeing nothing but gray shapes in the mist. Blue barked again, and I turned the water off and opened the shower door, a cloud of steam coming with me into the room.

Another bark, a "hello," a "there is someone here," a "someone we trust" bark. Grabbing a towel off the rack I left the bathroom, making wet prints on the carpeting as I padded through the bedroom into the living room. Blue sat by the door, his large tail swishing back and forth.

He barked again, turning to look at me, his mismatched eyes bright with excitement. He pushed his large head against my hip, urging me toward the door with a soft whine.

Mulberry stood in the hallway, his broad shoulders taking up the width of the doorway. He wore a subdued yellow and green plaid shirt that brought out the same colors in his eyes. Black stubble glittering with copper, gold, and silver covered his jaw.

Blue pushed past me and wriggled his body against Mulberry's legs. The former New York detective broke his gaze from mine and looked down at my dog. He ruffled Blue's head. "Hey, boy."

"I wasn't expecting you."

Mulberry looked up at me, his hand still on Blue. "That's the first thing you say?"

"Hi."

He smiled and gave off a little laugh. "I figured I'd stop by and see you. We left things a little ..."

"I thought I was pretty clear."

"I'm not sure it's entirely up to you to decide."

"I'm not sure about having this conversation in a towel."

Mulberry raised an eyebrow. "I don't think you need it."

"Come on in; I'll get dressed."

He followed me into the living room, clicking the door into place.

I dressed in a pair of dark, indigo jeans and a white T-shirt, one of the few I had without any stains. Blue's tail wagged and his tongue lolled out. "Don't look so excited," I told Blue before returning to the living room.

Mulberry waited on the couch. "You want a drink?"

"Sure."

I crossed to the small kitchenette and grabbed us each a bottle of sparkling water; cracking one open, it released that fizzing sound.

Mulberry came up behind me and placed his hand on my hip. I turned to him and opened my mouth to protest, but he shook his head.

He stepped closer so that our bodies brushed. His face was right above mine, his chin angled down, as I stared at his collarbones.

He fisted the short locks at the base of my skull and pulled gently so that my chin rose and our lips touched. His kiss was achingly familiar and electrifyingly new. The smell of him brought back memories I was afraid to face.

The pain of my brother's murder lanced through me; the paleness of his skin, the vivid red of his blood as he died—the gaping wound his loss left in me.

Everybody I love ends up dead. And not some gentle kiss into the night. They leave this world in violence and suffering; they end in misery.

I couldn't watch Mulberry die.

Was the pain of loving him and denying him worse than the ache I feared?

Mulberry's hand squeezed my hip, pressing our bodies together. His heart thumped so hard that I felt it against my breasts. Light danced behind my closed lids. My hands ran over his strong shoulders, caressing the corded muscles, before curving around his neck, intertwining and pulling at him.

Everything about it felt right, except for the consequences.

Mulberry's hands slipped under my shirt and he groaned against my mouth as the rough callouses of his fingers found my bare flesh.

"Stop thinking so much." His lips moved against my neck.

"I'm trying to be smart."

He laughed, his breath hot against my shoulder. "You've never been good at that."

"Hey."

"You're all instinct." A shiver ran from his lips over my skin. "You're overthinking this thing." I closed my eyes and relished the way we fit, the familiarity and the danger, the tugging of my heart toward him. This love wasn't a controllable force. "Stop trying to keep us all safe, Sydney."

"I have to."

He brought his head up, his steady gaze held mine. "You have to keep yourself safe."

"I'm—"

His eyes narrowed as my voice failed me. He shook his head and smiled a lazy, sexy grin. "You're not going to prison. Only a fool would waste an asset like you."

"What?" Fear spiked through me. "How do you know?" Blue was whining. "Just a minute, Mulberry." I shook him and he just kept up that grin, that all knowing, glinting-eyed smile.

Blue's whine pitched up.

"Stop!" I yelled, rolling over, my sheets tangled around me.

I stared across the expanse of the king-sized bed at Blue, who stood next to it, a soft whine pulling me fully out of the dream. The height of a Great Dane, with the coat of a wolf and the long, regal snout of a Collie, Blue had one blue eye and one brown. His eyebrows were raised and pushed together, creating a crease at the top of his long snout. He was worried about me.

I relaxed into the pillows, staring up at the ceiling. Just me and Blue were in the room. Mulberry was thousands of miles away.

My dreams were getting more vivid. The soft rumble of thunder sent a shiver of panic through me.

I didn't look at the window, not wanting to see that the sky was blue and the Pacific Ocean placid. Not wanting confirmation that my mind was tricking me, again. That I was broken, delusional. Crazy.

I threw off the blankets. Blue pranced happily and licked at my bare knee as I crossed the room to my chest of drawers and pulled out jogging clothes. Blue swung his tail, tapping his feet with excitement.

I shook my head, trying to dispel the unease that throbbed in my body.

I didn't bother with a leash for Blue. Here on the island, it wasn't necessary. I took the elevator down to the ground level and made my way through the warren of passages that led to the outside. Pushing through the final door, the sun glared into my eyes and I squinted against it.

Would this be one of the last times I saw the sun? Would Declan Doyle lock me in a cell without windows? I looked down at Blue and my chest tightened. How could I leave him?

Blue stayed at my hip as I walked along the dirt path. It wound around the volcano. The trail was over thirty miles long so I usually just jogged out for five miles and then back.

I broke into an easy run, my limbs warming up. The day wasn't hot yet, just very warm, the air moist and salty. As we came out from under the tree covering, the Pacific Ocean glittered in front of us. Blue touched his nose to my hip. Did he know how beautiful it was? Even in his black-and-white vision, was the ocean awe-inspiring?

I picked up my pace and the trail curled around the mountainside, the volcano rising to my right, and an almost sheer cliff of black, volcanic rock that ended in the Pacific Ocean to my left. Waves slapped against the rocks, spraying white foam.

The island was the headquarters of Joyful Justice, the vigilante network named after my birth name, Joy Humbolt.

Dan Burke, our head of operations, purchased the island from the estate of a billionaire. A prepper, paranoid about the fate of the world, he'd designed and constructed a safe haven that could house almost a hundred people, inside the inactive volcano.

Now, the basement levels were used for our headquarters, and the top floors were housing. This was where all of the missions for Joyful Justice were planned and led from.

Most of the people who lived and worked here didn't know I was the inspiration for the organization. I faked Joy's death years ago, hoping to end the fascination with her, but all I did was make her a martyr. Now, Declan Doyle, a former New York Police detective and current Homeland Security asshat was blackmailing me, threatening to reveal my true identity and other secrets about my past.

I picked up my pace, my feet pounding against the soft, dirt path, my breath long and steady, my muscles beginning to burn. Blue sprinted ahead of me, looking back over his shoulder, his tongue lolling out, his smile infectious. The pure delight he experienced on a run was half the reason I did it. The other half was to steady my mind and keep myself sane. Too bad it wasn't working the way that it used to.

My trainer, Merl, taught me to run when he first met me. When I was sprinting, my lungs fighting for air, my muscles on fire, there was no room in my head for questions or fear. It was just me in my body, racing.

Blue barked and I picked up my pace, legs flying, extending to their full length. We came around a bend; the wind whipping off the ocean kicked my hair around my face so that it stung my cheeks. Blue barked and I slowed. Someone was coming in the opposite direction.

Merl's three Dobermans came charging down the path with him close behind. He wore his long, tightly curled, black hair up in a bun. Mirrored aviators sat on his nose.

We both came to a stop as the dogs greeted each other. The path was narrow here and a frisson of fear jostled me as the dogs pranced around each other. Of course, they could handle it; they knew where the edge was. They knew how far to push it. I wish I shared their insights.

"Good morning," Merl said. I returned the greeting, the "good" sticking in my throat. "You okay?" Merl took off his glasses. His big brown eyes framed by thick lashes caught my gaze.

"Sure, yeah. I just didn't sleep well."

Merl nodded slowly. "You sure? You've been kind of off lately."

I looked away from him. The wounds on Merl's wrist had healed, leaving fat, red scars. He'd recently been imprisoned himself, taken hostage in China while trying to rescue his love, Mo Ping. I'd saved him —the way that he had always saved me.

Could he help me now? Was there any help for me?

"How is Mo Ping?" I asked, changing the subject, looking out to the sea, hiding from him.

"She's good. Are you?" Merl reached out and touched my forearm, trying to get me to look at him. I kept my gaze averted. "Are you seeing things again?"

Merl knew what it was to love from afar; he'd spent years pining after Mo Ping before admitting his feelings. I could tell him about Mulberry. That was safe. "I dreamed about Mulberry last night."

Merl nodded, his lips set with empathy.

"Why don't you go to Costa Rica? Go see him." Mulberry was at our training camp deep in the Central American jungle half-way around the world. Merl was headed back there soon himself. If I hadn't promised to meet Declan Doyle in Tokyo so that he could lock me up in exchange for keeping my secrets, I'd have that option.

"Maybe I will," I lied.

"You could use a break. You've been going nonstop."

I nodded and looked over at him. Merl smiled, raising his eyebrows, trying to remind me that we were friends, that I could trust him.

"I'll see you at the council meeting today." I started to move past him.

"Sure, sounds good."

I picked up my pace again, just a gentle run. Blue tapping his nose rhythmically against my hip. Mulberry's kiss flirted through my mind and his words resounded inside my skull.

An asset? I stopped running, my feet freezing to the ground. Of course! I might not know when thunder was real, but I was an asset. Declan would be a fool to lock me up and throw away the key. There were things I could do that no one else on the planet could, connections I had that no one else did, and that made me way too important to disappear. I turned around and ran back toward Merl, his dogs alerting him to my approach. Merl turned and cocked his head in question.

I was out of breath when I reached him. "Merl, there is something I've got to tell you."

$$EK$$

We sat in Dan's office, five stories underground, overlooking the headquarters of Joyful Justice. Through the interior window, I could see the wall of screens and banks of desks facing it. There were no active missions at the moment, but the screens displayed several aerial shots, places we were watching, reconnaissance missions.

I had just finished telling them about the deal I had made with Declan Doyle. Doyle was a New York City cop when I first met him and was now an important operative for Homeland Security. He was the only person in authority who knew my secrets—that Sydney Rye was Joy Humbolt; that Joy the Martyr was thus still alive; and that it was Bobby Maxim, not Joy, who killed the mayor of New York City—the celebrated act that had made Joy an inspiration to so many.

Maxim had tried unsuccessfully to assassinate Doyle. Now Doyle was threatening to expose the truth about Joy/Sydney, destroying the mythology at the core of Joyful Justice, if I didn't turn myself in to him and go to prison for my various crimes.

"So, you're telling me that Declan Doyle isn't dead," Dan said. His sun-bleached, brown hair was long, and he pushed it out of his eyes as he sat forward, his back to his desk that was covered in computer monitors. Merl and I sat on the black, leather couch, facing him. Our dogs lounged around the office, Blue by my feet, his eyes closed and breath even.

"That's right. He killed the assassin Robert Maxim sent after him and then made his offer to me."

Dan sat back in his chair; it creaked under his weight. He was over six feet tall, and pure wiry muscle. He led a stand-up paddleboard group four days a week, his way of getting the "computer nerds" out of the basement. His light-green eyes seemed even brighter against the dark tan of his skin.

"And you waited a week to tell us this?" Dan raised his eyebrows. A host of accusations were in that one sentence: you don't trust us, you're not a team player, you don't love me.

"It just occurred to me that he's not going to lock me up."

"I agree with her," Merl said. "I'm sure that Homeland Security wants something from her. Otherwise, there would be no reason to keep it secret. They'd want to announce her capture."

"So? What do you want to do?" Dan asked.

I was surprised he wasn't giving me more shit. Then again, maybe he'd finally realized what I was capable of. Or, more to the point, not capable of.

Dan and I had spent about six months together enjoying something very similar to love. Living in a small bungalow in Goa, India, he tended a garden and smoked hash while I read paperback novels. We shared a deep intimacy during that time, something I'd never had before, or since. The memory of his touch gave me strength. Dan was gentle and firm, strong and vulnerable: a wonderful man. It was the simplest my life had been since my brother's murder. The most peaceful. But, I couldn't live that way. There was no simple happiness for me. Unfortunately for Dan.

"I think we should let her go, and see how it plays out," Merl said. "You can track her, stay in touch. I don't think having a working relationship with Homeland Security is a terrible idea."

Dan shook his head. "No, it's a great idea." He turned to his computer for a moment. "I'll put a tracking beacon in Blue's collar." Blue raised his head at the sound of his name. "I've been working on something new that will allow me not only to track you, but also pick up on any communication devices near you and patch into them. So even if they take your cell, which I'm sure they will, we'll still be able to communicate."

"Wait, what? How is that possible?"

Dan looked over his shoulder at me and grinned. He was making fun of me and I smiled back, because I liked it when he teased. "Do you really want me to try and explain it to you?"

I shook my head. "I don't need to know the details of your genius, Dan. Just how I can use the damn thing."

He laughed. "Basically," he turned back around, crossing his foot over his thigh, "the beacon will allow me to patch into any cell phone or other form of communication device near you. So you're holding a walkie-talkie, I can cut in. You're with someone who has a cell phone, I can call you on it. Or just patch into the line."

"That's pretty cool."

"Actually," he grinned. "It's revolutionary."

"A revolutionary idea for a revolutionary. That works."

Merl's eyebrows conferred above his nose. "Sydney, I want to ask you something and I want you to be really honest with me." Lightning sizzled at the edge of my vision. I knew what he was going to ask and I knew that I would lie. "Are you seeing things?"

The lightning leapt across my vision and danced on the ceiling. I smiled. "Don't worry, I'm all good."

CHAPTER TWO

A week later, as I followed Declan Doyle's broad back down a fluorescent-lit hallway in the bowels of the Tokyo airport, I almost hoped we'd have to fight. He was a worthy opponent, but one I knew I could take. Taking Declan Doyle actually sounded like a lot of fun.

Declan wore the same ensemble he'd donned on our first date about five years earlier; a white dress shirt, the sleeves rolled up, top button left open, dark jeans that hugged him in all the right places, and a gold watch on his wrist—inherited from his grandfather.

He'd intercepted me in baggage claim—leaning against a wall, all casual. That chestnut-brown hair of his kicking off gold highlights in the sun streaming through the plate glass.

"I thought we'd agree you'd come alone."

I smiled. "You didn't really expect that, did you?"

"You can't take Blue with you where you're going."

"Oh," I frowned a little, holding Declan's gaze. "I'm pretty sure I can do whatever I want."

He smiled, but a light blush crept up his open collar. "I'm calling the shots here Sydney."

The baggage claim area was huge, about ten carrousels spilling luggage out. People were filtering in, others waited, some struggled with their bags. Children, adults, geriatrics, so many people totally unaware of the conversation happening in this little corner of the room.

"We both know I'm not here to turn myself in."

"You're not?"

A grin pulled at my lips. "You're not going to waste an asset like me, Declan." I held his gaze. His eyes were the same, deep brown they'd always been, his skin showed a few more lines, but the man was still devilishly handsome. Devilish being the primary term there.

"You need me."

"Need you?" His eyebrows rose again.

I shrugged. "Is 'want' a better term? I'm sure that Homeland Security has everything under control. Perhaps you just 'want' someone like me to help with your dirty work."

His smile faltered.

I stepped closer to Declan, leaving only a few inches between us. Blue stayed at my hip. "I know what I'm worth, Declan. And I'm ready to play."

The room Declan led me to was white, either freshly painted or rarely used. A white, plastic table with four chairs sat at its center. I glanced around, looking for the two-way mirror, but didn't see it.

In the upper corners, I spotted small cameras. "Have a seat." Declan pulled out a chair for me.

I dropped my small duffel at my feet and sat. Blue took up position on my left side, his chin hovering just above the table. I placed a hand on his back, rubbing between his shoulder blades. Declan sat across from me. "The camera's on?" I asked glancing up at the recording devices.

Declan shook his head.

"I was never here."

"Basically."

"So what do you want?"

"Always straight to the point."

I leaned back, stretching my hands over my head, reveling in the pull on my sides.

Blue yawned, his giant jaw unhinging, exposing large, sharp teeth.

"Long flight," I said with a smile as I lowered my hands.

"Tell me about Joyful Justice operating systems." Declan leaned back, leaving one hand—the one with the gold watch— resting on the table.

"What does that mean?"

"Who's in charge?" He flipped the hand over and back.

"No one."

"Okay." He shrugged one shoulder. "Who are the players?"

"You don't know?"

"Answer the question."

"I'm not telling you shit about Joyful Justice." I leaned forward, quickly. Declan didn't flinch and I smiled.

Blue let out a low, almost inaudible growl. A warning that my movement was merely a prelude to our joint attack.

"I'm here because you need something from me, and it's not information. No one comes to me for facts or details. I'm not the strategist, and you know that. You know me, Declan." I sat back in the chair. "So tell me what you want me to do. And I'll let you know if it's possible. Then we can each go our separate ways." Declan didn't move. "Or maybe you want more time with me for personal reasons? You did always like me."

Declan shook his head, his eyes burning. Anger? "You'll answer my questions, or I'll expose you."

"Bullshit. Where's your boss?"

"My boss?" He smiled.

"You have one, don't you? This is, after all, a J.O.B for you, Declan. You're not the head honcho."

"Head honcho?"

"Stop stalling."

Declan placed his large forearms on the table—dark hair over tan skin, that gold watch glinting at me, reminding me of his power—but I wasn't impressed.

Not anymore.

It took a lot more than strong arms and fine things to get me to react.

"I want information about Joyful Justice. And you're going to give it to me. Then we will discuss what you're going to do for me."

I bent forward, letting my forearms touch his—an electric charge heated me and a flicker of lightning danced in the corner of the room, flashing so fast I hardly saw it.

"Either lock me up," I smiled, feeling thunder rumbling in my veins, the aftershock of that twist of opposing ions, "or tell me what you want. I'm not giving you any information. If you thought I was going to, then you severely misunderstood the situation. The whole reason I'm here is to keep information hidden, not let more leak out. Duh."

He barked out a laugh. "This isn't a game. You're in the custody of Homeland Security and you're going to give us what we need."

"I'm not giving you shit, Declan. I'm not even here. So how long does this pissing match need to go on before you get to the point?"

Declan looked over at Blue. "We have ways of making you talk."

"Are you threatening my dog?" I asked, my voice low and dangerous. "I hope you're not threatening Blue. That never ends well."

Before Declan could answer, the door opened. A woman in her late forties with blonde hair cut into a neat bob, wearing a navy skirt suit tailored to her trim figure, entered.

She crossed the small space and offered me her hand. "Mary Leventhal." I stood and we shook: strong grips but not man-crushing, proving-shit hard. "Let us have the room, Doyle."

I smiled. So, here was his boss—a woman.

Declan rose, his chair legs scraping against the floor. I watched him go, looking for that blush I loved so much, but it didn't appear. He didn't mind her taking control. Classic Declan: He liked a strong woman—until he didn't.

Mary sat down across from me. "Please." She indicated the seat I'd vacated. Blue sniffed the air, getting a taste of her. "Incredible dog. I'd heard of him, but I don't think the pictures do him justice."

"Sure."

She smiled at me—politician, friend, ally—it said all in one splitting of lips. "You're right. We do need something from you, and it's not information. Though we'd like that too."

I didn't answer.

"Sydney Rye, aka Joy Humbolt. Seems your alias is in almost as much trouble as your birth name."

"I didn't know there were any warrants out for me."

"The intelligence community is aware of your role in Joyful Justice."

"You're Declan's boss."

"Superior."

"Oh, I like that even better. So what's your official title?"

"Do you need to know that?"

I shrugged. "I guess not, why? Don't you have one? Or is this whole thing off books, including you?"

It was her turn to shrug. "I'm here for one reason and one reason only. I'm here to recruit you. I think we can work together."

"You and me or our organizations."

"Both. I hope that we will have a long and fruitful relationship."

"You're going to scratch my back?"

"I have information about possible targets that I think your organization would love to get a hold of. I'm willing to offer my help in exchange for yours."

"I'm listening."

"There are a lot of rules when you're the most powerful nation on the planet."

"And here I thought if you were the biggest bully on the playground, you got to do whatever you wanted."

Mary frowned. "You think we're in a playground? I might have overestimated you. Perhaps Declan is blind to your true personality due to your personal connection. But he told me you were smart and ruthless."

"I wouldn't deny either of those attributes."

"Then obviously you recognize the incredible complications involved in international relations."

"I'm not good at relationships. I'm better at blowing shit up. Both literally and figuratively."

"Then let me be straight with you. What we are looking for is to have you blow some shit up that we can't."

I smiled. "I like it when you talk like that, Mary." She couldn't quite keep the smile off her lips, but it only flashed for a moment. "Why don't you tell me what you want exploded, and I'll let you know if I can do it."

Mary nodded. "Daesh."

"Daesh. As in the Islamic State? As in the guys who control a goodly portion of Iraq and Syria?"

"Yes, I want you to help kill their leadership." I didn't respond. "They've taken thousands of women captive."

I recognized the cold anger in her expression. It matched mine. The story of the women Daesh brutalized and controlled hurt in our bones—in our very marrow. They were the perfect example of our sex's vulnerability—what men always had over us.

"And killing their leaders is going to help? Won't more just pop up in their place?"

"You don't want to do it?"

"Look," I put my forearms back on the table. "One of the things we do at Joyful Justice is let the injured, the wronged, bring us cases. We don't just go in and start fucking with random situations. See, cause that's how you get a Daesh."

"Excuse me?"

"If the USA in all its school-bully wisdom had never gone into Iraq, Daesh wouldn't even exist. Fighting for freedom, for rights, for anything, has to be done—at least in part—by the people who are going to benefit."

Mary nodded. "Exactly. That's why I want you to work with the FKP. Kurdish female freedom fighters. There is nothing Daesh fighters hate more than getting killed by a woman. They think it keeps them out of Heaven."

"Work with them how?"

"You're an inspiration."

I laughed. "Don't go blowing smoke up my ass. I'm no such thing."

"Joy Humbolt is."

"She's dead."

"Martyrs make the best inspiration. Didn't you know that when you killed her?"

"No. I was hoping I'd leave her behind."

Mary looked me over, slowly. "You're unrecognizable. And it's not just the scars." I felt the ruined flesh tingle when she mentioned it. They'd faded over the last five years but were still obvious; a dark line under my left eye tightened the skin across my cheekbone. Another scar over that same eye sliced through my eyebrow, across my temple, and disappeared into my hairline. I wore bangs to cover it but the scars were a reminder every time I looked in the mirror of what bad men will do if you don't stop them. "You were a girl, and now you're a killer."

I raised my eyebrows. "You can just look at a person and tell?"

"Can't you?"

I assessed Mary for a moment: hard, blue eyes, controlled movements, even breathing. She'd killed before and could do it again, and with the right weapon it probably wouldn't even wind her. I nodded in answer to her question.

"I'm offering you the opportunity to do what you love. Go after the worst kind of scum, the darkest, most foul dredges of humanity."

"Guys you can't go after."

"It's not that I can't. We can kill them—we have. Drones are a powerful weapon. But like you said, more just pop up in their place. We are losing the more important battle."

"Hearts and minds."

"Exactly. Young, Muslim men are pouring out of the Western World and going to fight for Daesh. Do you know why? It's the same reason people are joining Joyful Justice. They want to believe they are involved in something worth fighting for. They want their lives to mean something—to matter."

"Even if I am some kind of 'inspiration,'" I used air quotes (which I hardly ever do but if you're referring to yourself as an inspiration and you don't use hand quotes then your ego probably needs a punch in the balls), "I'm already dead, so how can I inspire all over again?"

"You can help, trust me." She leaned forward, her suit moving flawlessly with her. "And, I don't mean to sound like I'm pressuring you here. But it's not like you have a choice." She smiled.

I smiled slowly back at her. "Oh, Mary, don't you know, you always have a choice?"

"Do those women Daesh is holding?"

"Everyone has a choice. They choose to live. I respect it."

"They could chose to die?"

"That's often an option."

"What are your other options right now?"

"I could leave."

She shook her head. "No, you can't. It's this or we're going to lock you up."

"And you say you're not a bully."

"Bullies don't lock you up. They take your lunch money. I'm talking about solitary confinement." She looked over at Blue. "As in all alone."

I shook my head. "I feel like I just had this conversation. The one where I made it clear threatening my dog was a real, real bad idea."

"I'm not threatening your dog. I'm threatening you. With incarceration." Her gaze held mine.

I smiled and let out a small laugh. "You know something, Mary?"

"Hmmm?"

"I like you."

"Glad to hear it. Now, let's get to work on your assignment."

"Assignment. Does that make me a spy?"

"Like you said, Sydney: You're an asset. A very important asset."

CHAPTER THREE

It was night when we landed in Kurdish-controlled Iraq. The lack of light pollution let the cosmos come out and play. The Milky Way curved above us, all those stars forming a band of light across the black sky. The hugeness of the Universe was much more obvious here than in the light-polluted clouds over Tokyo.

The war waging in the mountains that surrounded us could almost be thought of as insignificant if you let your mind open to the vastness of space. Nothing smaller than a planet could seem big in that wide an angle.

But as our plane landed, the wheels making contact with the smooth pavement of the runway built by American money thousands of miles away from our own soil, this conflict could seem like the center of it all. Certainly, it was for this region.

And all of it was so stupid—so important and so fucking stupid. Fighting over how other people should live. Common sense didn't exist here. The golden rule was twisted into nightmare proportions.

Waging war because of the words in a dead religious tome—one that was interpreted by each sect differently—so much death and misery because of one fucking book.

As we taxied under that big, beautiful sky I tasted the rotten flavor of hypocrisy in my mouth. It was zealotry that fueled this wasteful massacre of humanity. It was zealotry that got my butt in this seat.

I was as uncompromising in my pursuit of justice as the men hiding in the hills were about their warped interpretation of Islam. They took their ideas from a book; it made them confident they had the right to treat women as objects to be covered, or violated, to leave their seed inside them, to force them to do whatever they wanted. I didn't have a book, but I had faith in my right to kill every last one of them.

Mary unclipped her seatbelt and stood. "Ready."

I grabbed my bag, and with Blue by my side, deplaned onto that flawless tarmac glowing black under the light of the Universe.

The air smelled of burning plastic and crisp mountains. Blue touched his nose to my hip, reminding me he was there. I laid a hand on his head as a Humvee approached our small plane. Declan came and stood next to me. "You ready for this?"

I craned my neck slightly to look up at him. He was watching the Humvee. "I was born ready."

He glanced at me and smiled. Two figures climbed out of the vehicle. They were women wearing sand-colored uniforms that hid their curves.

Mary greeted them in Kurdish. She turned to me. "Sydney Rye, this is Sergeant Sazan Rashid and Private Mujada Taib. They are going to be working with you. Sergeant Rashid is your translator and Private Taib is your bodyguard."

My translator took my hand. "It's a pleasure to meet you, Ms. Rye." Her accent was elegant, lyrical, like her native tongue.

"Thank you; I look forward to working with you."

Private Taib stepped forward. She was bigger than Sazan by about four inches, her shoulders broad, and her jaw square. "Good to meet you."

She grunted at my greeting.

"Private Taib doesn't have much English," Mary said. "But she's very good at her job."

"I have no doubt."

Blue tapped his nose to my hip. "This is Blue. He's my other bodyguard." I smiled at the women, trying to look friendly. They both looked at Blue, seeming surprised that I'd introduced him.

"Shall we go?" Declan asked, waving his arm toward the Humvee.

We climbed aboard—Mary, Declan, Blue and I in the back seat, the two Kurds in the front—Private Taib behind the wheel.

The mountains around us rose sharply into the starry sky. The hillsides were barren except for scrub brush that seemed to thrive on the sharp angles and dry climate.

Our headlights cut through the darkness, illuminating the blacktop. The tires droned over it, audible above the aggressive, mechanical rasp of the engine. Blue leaned against my leg, his body transferring heat through my cargo pants. I played with one of his ears, running my fingers over the velvety fur.

Mujada slowed the vehicle as our headlights hit the blackened crater of an explosion. The pavement was peeled back, large slabs of it angled toward the sky, raising up around a deep pit. She veered onto the dirt shoulder, maneuvering around the destroyed section of the road.

"An IED," Sazan said in explanation. "But don't worry," she turned in her seat flashing a smile. "There shouldn't be any more. This area has been secure for some time now."

I caught Mujada's eyes in the rearview mirror. Her eyelashes were long and thick, irises black in the low light. Charcoal edged her lids, adding to the drama of her gaze. Mujada broke eye contact as she steered the large vehicle back onto the blacktop.

As the road curved around a steep mountainside, it split and Mujada took the left fork. In the distance, a low, large structure was visible. It was a walled compound, the same dusty brown as the hillsides around it. The shadow it threw was pure black.

At the tall, solid metal entrance gate two female soldiers waited. They wore helmets and flak jackets and carried rifles. Dark figures patrolled the top of the wall. Two mounted machine guns pointed down at us.

Mujada opened her window and spoke briefly with one of the soldiers. The gate rolled open on well-oiled bearings.

Sazan pointed at a building in front of us. "That's the mess hall and meeting rooms." She pointed to three other smaller structures to her right. "The barracks." Gesturing to the left to more low buildings, Sazan explained, "More barracks and training facilities. The armory is also that way."

Mujada parked in front of the mess hall.

Blue jumped out ahead of me, and, stretching his neck, he raised his nose to the air and sniffed.

Several female soldiers stood on the inside of the entrance gate. Their expressions were hard to read in the darkness, but their eyes were trained on Blue and me. Mary climbed out of the Humvee and stood next to me, following my gaze.

"They look curious," I said.

"Wouldn't you be?"

"I'm always curious, Mary, that's what gets me into trouble."

"Or makes you great." Mary started toward the mess hall. Mujada stood next to the Humvee, waiting for me to go ahead of her.

Blue and I followed Mary, Mujada stepping in behind us. Her large, solid presence was comforting in a way I hadn't expected. Was it her even breathing? Or steady steps? Or perhaps the slight turn down of her lips, the permanent frown of concentration, that made me feel secure?

I glanced over my shoulder at the woman who was responsible for protecting me (and possibly confining me) in this place. Her body was tense and her eyes scanned the environment. Did she suspect an attack from outside? Or was it the people inside the compound that she feared?

The mess hall was filled with long, wooden tables lined with chairs; the scent of old fryer grease and coffee lingered in the air. Vinyl posters with grainy photographs hung from the rafters.

"Are you hungry?" Sazan asked as the door closed behind us. The room was mostly empty, just a few women scattered around in groups of three and four. "We have tea, coffee, water."

"Water for me and Blue."

Sazan turned to Mary, who asked for a cup of coffee; Declan wanted coffee too. Sazan gestured for us to pick a table and headed toward the kitchen to retrieve our drinks. After we sat down, Declan took a long look around the room. "It's amazing; all women."

"So amazing," Mary drawled in a mocking tone.

"You don't think so?"

"I just don't think it's as shocking as you do."

"I didn't say it was shocking." Declan's eyebrows rose. "I think it's something I've never seen before. It's unusual." He looked over at me. "I think it's incredibly powerful."

Women made up the majority of the ranks of Joyful Justice, so mess halls with few men present didn't seem unusual to me. A community of women does have a different energy though; the underlying aggression in male-dominated environments is absent, but like all camps in war zones, there was a strong sense of community.

This was a sisterhood rather than a brotherhood—the fierceness with which these soldiers fought was equal to those of their male counterparts. However, at the root of the fight was a different engine; women are physically the weaker sex; denying that is like denying that Blue has one blue eye and one brown. We are smaller, our upper bodies will never have the strength of the strongest men, and we can be violated in a way that no man can.

Men can be raped, of course, but they cannot be impregnated. No one can forcibly plant the seed of life inside a man.

However, despite those obvious physical weaknesses, women have a strength that men do not. There is a reason we are the ones who bear children. Because we can *bear* them, physically and emotionally.

What does all that add up to? Women are different from men: Our strength lies in our emotional intelligence and our empathy rather than in brute strength.

"Whose idea was this?" I asked Mary.

"What do you mean?"

"This place, the all-female fighting force. Was this your idea?"

Mary smiled. "I wish. This is a part of the Kurdish-Iraqi mindset. They're socialists. They believe in equality of the sexes."

"Interesting that they're so equal, yet separate. Separate but equal doesn't always work out the way it's supposed to. In fact, I don't think it ever has."

The door opened and I felt Mujada tense next to me. We were facing the entrance, our backs to the rest of the room. Blue sat behind me, covering the part of the room I could not see.

Three women walked in, laughing. Their dark hair was pulled back into high ponytails. They were slim and fit and at the very beginning of their adult lives. On their waists, they carried pistols, knives, and extra ammo.

"Everyone is armed all the time here?"

"Looks that way," Declan replied.

I turned to Mujada. "Do you speak any English?"

"A little," she answered, her accent thick, her voice a lovely, rich, gravel tone.

"Everyone wear a gun all the time?"

She shrugged and did not reply, her eyes drifting back to the entrance.

Sazan returned. She passed a steaming mug to Declan and another to Mary before sliding two bottles of water across the table to me.

I opened my small duffel and removed Blue's travel bowl. Made of waterproof canvas, it folded flat for easy storage. I filled it with water and placed it on the floor in front of Blue so he could drink and continue to watch his side of the room.

"Everyone is always armed here?" I asked Sazan.

She nodded. "It seems like the safest option."

"So do you have weapons for us?"

Sazan nodded. "Yes, of course. In the morning when the armory opens, we will get you whatever you need."

I surveyed the room, my gaze falling on the posters hanging from the rafters. Each rectangle featured three grainy photographs, the head and shoulders of women. "What's up with the posters?"

"They are martyrs," Mary answered. Her tone made me glance at her; there was a smile on her lips—she knew something I didn't.

"Yes," Sazan agreed. I scanned the posters, looking at each, pixilated image—most of the women had dark hair and serious expressions. "This is the newest one." Sazan was pointing at a poster to our left; it featured only one woman. She had fierce eyes, a grim expression, and scars on her neck. "The Tigress. She was a great leader of the FKP. Daesh claims to have killed her."

"Claims?" I asked.

"They posted a video beheading a woman. But many believe it was not the Tigress. That she is still alive, out there hunting Daesh."

"The FKP has ties to Iran," Mary said to me. "If you remember from your briefing."

I nodded, recalling the myriad of initialed organizations Mary had told me about. It was impossible to keep them all straight, and that wasn't just me. Mary admitted that they changed names and affiliations often. If a group calling itself FKP worked with Iran, accepting money and weapons, it didn't mean that another group, made up of the same members, but operating under different initials, wasn't working with the United States.

My gaze drifted to the furthest poster, a photograph of a blonde. I squinted, confusion hazing my vision and then the picture became clear, the whole thing suddenly obvious; it was Joy Humbolt. Thunder boomed and the hair on my arms rose as electricity sizzled in my veins.

EK

The room Sazan escorted Blue and me to had honey-colored, wood-paneled walls that reminded me of movies about summer camp. A single bed with a thin mattress, hard pillow, and a slate-gray, wool blanket shared the space with a small desk and chair.

I dropped my duffle on the bed and sat down next to it. Blue sat by my side and leaned into my leg, resting his head across my knees. I ran my finger over the soft fur between his eyes. He closed his lids and sighed appreciatively.

The sounds of the camp filtered through the closed window: laughter as a group's footsteps passed, along with the rustle of clothing and the swish of sleeves.

Still dressed, I stretched out on the bed and folded my hands on my chest staring up at the blank ceiling above me. Blue lay down next to the bed, his body facing the door, while my sights fell on the single window.

Exhausted, all I wanted was to fall asleep, but the posters of martyrs was unsettling. Especially seeing my own face up there, or at least the face of my past. While I'm all for honoring the dead, it's dangerous to hold them up as some kind of example. It's too easy to turn their lives, filled with all their reality, into a useful fiction.

The mythology of Joy Humbolt was a perfect example of that fiction. The people she inspired believed that she'd taken the law into her own hands when her brother was murdered by a man too powerful for law enforcement to touch. And that was indeed my intention. But in reality, I was too late. Robert Maxim, a man with even more influence, arranged his death, not to avenge my brother, but to protect his own interests.

There was nothing noble about what happened. Nothing worth replicating.

However, Joyful Justice was spawned from that fiction, and I believed in the organization and its mission. I'd always thought of it as inspiring people striving for their own goals: the sex slave fighting for her freedom, the mother battling for the environment her children lived in, communities eradicating the drugs that plagued their lives.

Here, Joy was a war hero.

I'm not talking about the "war against injustice," war in a metaphoric sense. These women were fighting for control of land and what kind of lives could be lived upon it.

A soft knock at my door and Blue was on his feet, nose pressed to the crack underneath it.

"Who is it?" Without a weapon to grab, I felt naked.

"Mujada."

I turned the deadbolt and opened the door. "Come with me." Her words were stilted but practiced.

"Why?"

She beckoned, crooking her fingers up and pulling them toward her palm. I glanced back at my duffle. Should I bring it with me? Mujada shook her head.

I grabbed Blue's leash and clipped it to his collar before following her down the hall. We stepped back out into the night and Mujada led me quickly across the road to a darkened building.

Retrieving a key from her pocket, Mujada opened the deadbolts and pulled the door wide. I stepped into the darkened room first. The sound of my boots on cement echoed. We were in a room with high ceilings. It smelled like oil and dust.

Mujada closed the door behind us and clicked on a flashlight. The light illuminated a polished, gray floor, then panned up, hitting the metal legs of storage shelves and exposing wooden crates with Kurdish letters stenciled across them in white spray paint. Mujada moved forward, Blue and I in her wake.

She passed the first shelving unit and turned down the next aisle.

My eyes struggled to adjust in the darkness because of the bright beam of the torch. I could sense that the shelves rose to the ceiling, which felt about twelve feet tall. Blue's nails clicked against the cement in time with the clunk of our boots.

Mujada stopped, and placing the flashlight between her shoulder and ear, she used both hands to open a crate at about chest height.

The light shook from her movements, but I could see that inside the crate, cushioned in black foam, were automatic rifles. The same make and model as the ones carried by the guards at the gate.

She pulled one out and handed it to me before retrieving another for herself. It smelled brand-new. Mujada replaced the lid and continued down the aisle.

The back wall of the building was lined with more shelves. Mujada scanned with her flashlight until it lit up boxes of ammunition. She grabbed two, handing them to me, and then took two more for herself.

Mujada turned back toward the door and picked up her pace as we headed to the exit.

We left the building, the machine guns on our backs, the shells in our hands. Mujada locked the door, turned off her flashlight, and gestured that we should return to the barracks.

Back in my bedroom, the door locked behind us, Mujada's big body resonated with tension. She went to the window and looked through the small gap in the curtains.

The room felt even smaller with the three of us in it. Mujada released the magazine from her rifle and began to fill it. I followed her lead.

The shells were beautiful; gold and smooth, about the length of my middle finger, pointed at the tip with a thin shaft that led to a thicker one. The low thrum of thunder purred as I ran the pad of my thumb over the grooved rings on the circular base.

We worked in silence, and when it was done, Mujada pushed her magazine home with a satisfying click before leaning against the wall and peering through the slit in the curtains.

She gestured for me to get in bed. I cocked my head. She pulled back the covers and patted her hand on the pillow.

I looked down at the weapon in my lap.

Why, surrounded by allied women in arms, did Mujada think it necessary that I not only cuddle up with a machine gun tonight but that I sleep with her standing above my head, armed and ready to defend me?

Blue was sitting on the floor watching Mujada, his tail swishing back and forth slowly.

I removed my shoes, keeping the cargo pants and shirt on, before stretching onto the bed. Mujada hit the lights. I rolled onto my side so that my back was to Mujada and Blue and the door.

I trusted them to protect me from the physical world. Could anyone save me from the deterioration of my mind?

CHAPTER FOUR

In the morning, Mujada was gone.

Blue stood and stretched, sticking his butt up in the air and waving his tail around, letting loose a big yawn that exposed his teeth all the way to his molars.

I stood and reached toward the ceiling stretching myself. Blue pushed against my hip with his nose and looked at the door, encouraging me to go for a run.

"I don't think this is the kind of place you go for a jog. I'll ask Sazan about it, though."

Blue yowled and tapped his feet, refusing to accept my explanation. "How about some breakfast first?"

I fed Blue and refilled his water.

Standing at the window, listening to Blue crunch on his kibble, I watched the base wake up. The sun exposed the landscape that the shadows of the night before had only hinted at. The base sat on a flat plain, the distant hillsides, rocky and steep formed a forbidding border. I'd thought the only vegetation was scrub brush, but in the morning light I could see thick forests of pine trees at higher altitudes. I'd expected a desert landscape, something devoid of life.

When Blue finished breakfast, I grabbed my toiletry bag and fresh clothing, heading down the hall. Blue waited outside as I showered quickly and put on clean, gray sweatpants, a white T-shirt, and a matching sweatshirt.

When I put on sneakers and clipped a leash to Blue's collar he got excited, vibrating with energy as we left the barracks. "We're not going running right now."

My statement did not damper his enthusiasm. As we moved through the brightening day toward the mess hall, his nose rhythmically tapped my waist.

I could hear the din of conversation from the steps of the dining room, and when I opened the door, the sound was amplified. Over a hundred women filled the space. They sat at the long tables talking and laughing, their cutlery smacking against plastic plates. A line snaked around the room to the buffet. I joined it and Blue scanned the room, his nostril's flaring.

The women were dressed in fatigues and combat boots, sidearms holstered on their hips. They were looking at us. Not all at once, but taking turns. Blue was the only dog, and I was the only person out of uniform in the room.

My gaze rose to the posters of the martyrs. Would I ever be comfortable or truly understand the role which Joy Humbolt played in the world?

Sydney Rye, with her discipline and strength and bravery, was so much more real to me than that blonde, sweet-looking girl who held a place of honor in this war zone.

The energy in the room shifted, and I turned to see Declan entering. He moved smoothly toward the line of women waiting for the buffet. Declan moved like a tiger lurking in the jungle, hiding with his stripes.

I waved to him and he smiled. We looked at each other, wondering about the protocol of cutting in line. It felt silly and somehow very high school. Maybe it was because most of these women were so young, their faces unlined and the pitch of their voices not yet fully matured.

I could see women blushing and turning to each other, whispering. I remembered my own reaction to Declan when I wasn't much older than the soldiers around us. It had been almost five years since Declan and I met. The transformation I'd undergone was shocking. It made me unrecognizable to the people in the room despite my picture hanging above their heads during every meal. Declan had hardly changed. The years had only added to his confidence.

I picked up a tray and felt Declan slide in beside me.

"Good morning."

"Morning."

"How'd you sleep?"

I glanced up at Declan and smiled. "Just fine. How about you?"

"Just fine."

We filled our trays with eggs and toast. I even got a little cup of oatmeal sprinkled with dates and honey.

Mary came in as we were finding a table and waved at us before joining the line for food.

"This is delicious," Declan said.

An explosion outside shook the building, raining dust down on us. Declan and I jumped to our feet. Blue pressed against my left leg. Another explosion sounded, this one closer. The soldiers abandoned their breakfast and were filing out quickly.

Mary joined us. "I don't think that was inside the walls."

"I think it was outside, but that doesn't mean it won't be inside soon." Declan responded.

I started for the door; Declan and Mary followed. Blue tapped my hip, his ears swiveling, nostrils flaring.

There was another boom. The abandoned plates rattled on the tables. "That one sounds closer," Mary said. I didn't waste time talking. "Where are you going?"

I pushed through the door, breaking into a jog.

Black smoke billowed on the other side of the main gate. The rat-tat of gunfire sounded.

"Where is Mujada?" Declan asked as he followed my pace.

I ran across the road and pushed into the barracks building. Unlocking my bedroom door, I strode the short distance to the bed, reaching underneath and pulling out the machine gun.

"Where did you get that?" Mary asked.

"Does it matter? Aren't you glad I have it?"

"Depends on how you plan to use it."

I smiled, "Don't worry. I'm not going to kill you. At least not today."

"Comforting," Mary said.

"You want one?"

They both nodded. I retrieved my duffel bag and pulled out my lock pick set. "Let's go get some."

Mary and Declan followed me out of the barracks and to the armory. Soldiers were running toward the entrance in formation. Their boots pounded on the ground, dust rising up behind them.

As we arrived at the armory, I handed my weapon to Declan. He smiled and turned his back to cover me while I dropped to my knees, pulled out the lock picking kit and went to work.

"Mujada!" I heard Mary yell.

I glanced over my shoulder. Mujada was running toward us, rifle in hand.

Returning my attention to the lock, I continued my ministrations. I'd never been a great lock pick, but with time and patience, I could get most doors open.

Another explosion sounded and the ground shook. My fingers slipped and I dropped one of my picks.

Mujada was speaking quickly in a mix of Kurdish and English to Mary who was asking her to slow down. Mujada's voice became more frustrated. I heard Blue growl as Mujada's hand clamped onto my shoulder. "Go now," she said.

"We need more weapons."

She handed her keys to Mary and grabbed my arm, pulling me onto my feet. Blue let out another warning growl. I resisted as she began to pull me down the road toward the back of the camp. "Hey!" I yelled planting my feet and trying to yank free from her.

Her fingers dug into my arm. Blue barked again, looking at me for guidance. Should I use him or follow her?

Mary had opened up the armory and was inside. Declan looked back and forth between the open doorway and Mujada and me. "Now!"

Mujada yanked me again, her gaze focused on the smoke floating down the street. The sound of gunfire was constant.

"Declan, give me my rifle!"

He hesitated only a moment before closing the space between us and passing it to me. Mujada kept her iron grip on my arm and continued to pull me. "Just a minute." I broke free from her but didn't make it far. The butt of Mujada's gun hit me on the temple. Searing pain was followed by total darkness.

EK

Consciousness returned with the sway and buck of a vehicle underneath me. I reached up to touch my temple and groaned. Blue licked my face and I blinked my eyes open.

It was dark; I was lying on metal. It was hot and the air stank of oil and gunpowder. Dark green canvas covered metal arches above me and benches lined the space. Sunlight shot through the holes where string tied the canvas to the struts. I realized I was in a troop transport vehicle.

But it was just me and Blue. I rolled onto my side and then pushed up on to all fours. *I'm going to puke.* Several deep breaths helped to contain my nausea.

Another fucking concussion. How many had I had now? As many as a football player? I almost laughed out loud. More brain damage—just what I needed.

Less than a year earlier, I was doused with a powerful hallucinogen, Datura. After wandering in the Everglades for days, with Blue keeping me alive, I spent weeks in a pliable state, completely divorced from myself, in a hospital. I had no memories from the experience. But a lot of residual trauma.

There'd been a storm while Blue and I were in the wild. The thunder and lighting, the wind and the rain, now seeped into my everyday life, wreaking havoc and threatening to undo me. But I wasn't giving up yet.

I grabbed onto one of the benches and hauled myself onto it, leaning against one of the metal struts supporting the canvas. Blue sat next to me, resting his weight against my left leg and placing his head across my knees.

I ran my hands down his flanks and over his legs, searching for injuries. He appeared to be unharmed.

I closed my eyes and took several deep breaths, concentrating on stopping the spinning sensation that was making me feel like I was stuck in an ocean wave. The low pulsating beat of thunder rose and fell with my lungs.

Sliding down the bench toward the back of the truck, I began to work on one of the corners of the canvas with fingers that trembled.

The cord was nylon and coated in a protective layer of plastic. I could not loosen it, so I pressed my eye up against one of the eyelets and tried to see out.

I caught flashes of dark-green pine forest and the red, muddy tracks of a road. My effort had revived the raging headache, so I sat back and closed my eyes.

Should I jump out? I had no idea where I was, no supplies and no weapons. Was it possible that the driver of this transport vehicle was friendly? I couldn't decide.

My instincts told me to trust Mujada. Blue had seemed to like her. So being kidnapped by her was confusing and not just because my head was spinning.

From the beginning, she'd appeared concerned with my safety, but was that just because she needed me alive for whatever this journey was? Or were Mary and Declan a threat to me in a way I had not yet recognized?

I decided to wait out the drive, figuring that if nothing else, when we arrived at our destination, I had a chance of obtaining a weapon and stealing a ride.

Blue whined softly and I opened my eyes. He scooted closer to me, pressing against my legs. In the darkness, his eyes reflected green.

"Why would you let them put us in here?"

No response.

The fact that Blue appeared uninjured made me think that it was possible that Mujada's intentions were pure.

I closed my eyes again and rested my head against the canvas, letting the bounce of the road lull me back into an uneasy sleep.

Blue woke me by licking my hand and my eyes shot open as we rolled to a stop.

"Showtime."

My legs were unsteady, but not unusable. I stood, knees bent, facing the back of the vehicle, waiting for our escort to arrive.

The nylon cord began to unravel, splitting the back of the canvas. Light came in slowly, creeping across the floor, touching the tip of my running shoes, slanting over the laces and up my ankles.

I braced myself, digging my toes in, my left leg forward, right back, ready to run and kick the shit out of whoever was on the other side of that canvas.

I blinked trying to adjust to the bright light. I could see a waist and chest. The person was wearing fatigues, the same ones all the women at the base camp had worn.

I guessed it was Mujada.

When she looked into the darkened space and saw us standing there, Blue's hackles raised and my hands up, both of us ready for a fight, Mujada held up her own palms and said, "Sorry."

"Sorry for what exactly?"

She frowned and I cursed the language barrier between us. "Is Sazan here?" I asked.

Mujada shook her head. Slowly lowering her hands she reached into a pant pocket. Blue growled a low warning as my body tensed.

She pulled out a small, fat, battered book. The cover was red and the title was white. She held it up so that I could read: Kurdish/English Dictionary.

"I wonder if kidnapping is in there."

Mujada thumbed through until she found the page she wanted.

"Danger for you."

"What kind of danger?"

Mujada thumbed some more, "I must protect you."

"Why?"

"The Tigress wants to meet you."

35

CHAPTER FIVE

I lowered my fists, the tension fading from my limbs, replaced by nausea. Mujada returned the book to her pocket and gestured for me to come out of the back of the truck.

Mujada's arm steadied me as I climbed down.

We were at the end of a dirt road. Tall pine trees surrounded us, their rich scent filling the air. The sky was blue with small, puffy, white clouds drifting across it. The sun was behind the trees and I guessed that it was about three o'clock.

Mujada led us to the front seat and pulled out two automatic rifles, passing one to me. I recognized them as the ones we'd lifted from the armory together.

The rifle gave me a sense of control and helped to ease the dizziness.

Mujada reached into the front seat and pulled out a backpack, handing it to me. I opened it up and found two water bottles and a couple of U.S. government-issued Meals Ready To Eat (MRE's).

Mujada pulled out another pack for herself and closed the door. She reached into her bag and showed me a bowl for Blue and his bag of kibble.

She hadn't forgotten him.

Mujada led the way, going around the truck, heading into the trees. I put the backpack over my shoulders and followed.

What had happened to Mary and Declan? Did Mujada hurt them?

I had never faced Mary in a physical fight, but Declan and I had squared off and I knew that he was a formidable opponent. And that was when he was up against somebody he cared about. I imagined he was incredibly dangerous when dealing with people he had no emotional connection to.

Mujada pushed back branches of underbrush and ducked under limbs, moving through the forest as if she were following a trail, but it all looked the same to me.

We walked for about an hour and the sun drifted lower, making the shadows in the forests longer, closer together, leaving less light for us to navigate by. Mujada stopped and pulled a bottle of water from her pack, drinking deeply from it.

I did the same, pouring some for Blue as well.

Blue lapped at the water, spilling it over the sides, darkening the dried pine needles at our feet. Mujada raised her fingers to her lips, asking if I was hungry.

The nausea had abated as we walked, so I nodded, immediately regretting the gesture, as pain and the rumble of thunder ricocheted through my head. Mujada pulled out a blanket; it was the same slate wool as the one that had been on my bed back at the camp, and laid it down, gesturing for me to sit.

It reminded me of the tea parties my brother, James, and I had hosted when we were children. Sitting in our backyard, the crab grass covered with the blanket from our parent's bed, we stuck out our pinkies and used English accents as we pretended to sip tea from plastic cups. Our honored guests, stuffed animals and transformers, formed a circle around us.

Mujada pulled out one of the ready-to-eat meals and passed it to me.

I took it and stared down at the package, my eyes stinging with tears.

How long ago did James and I play in that backyard? Twenty years ago? That was about right. The memory felt ancient and fresh: time a wavering line, folding onto itself, and stretching to infinite.

Blue sat behind me and leaned his body against my back. I rubbed his hind leg.

The thunder faded as I opened the MRE. It was chicken and rice. There was even a small packet of Tabasco sauce. The food was salty but filling and I ate it quickly, my appetite strong.

"The food for Blue."

Blue stood, ears and tail high.

Mujada cocked her head at me. I made the same fingers to mouth eating motion she'd used and pointed to Blue. She smiled and nodded before pulling out his kibble and dumping some into his empty water bowl.

Blue looked at me and I nodded, sending new peals of thunder through my brain and fissures of lighting radiating at the edge of my vision.

Blue crunched on the kibble, looking up between bites, scanning the forest around us, his ears twitching back and forth.

A bird landed on the tree limb above us and let out a short burst of song before taking flight, the branch shaking slightly from its exit. The forest was thick, wild, and healthy. It seemed far away from any battlefield.

Our meal finished, Mujada repacked the blanket and our empty MRE containers. Before we started on our trek, Mujada rearranged the pine needles, hiding all signs that two women and a dog had picnicked there.

We continued walking, stopping about every hour to drink water and sit in companionable silence. Jogging sneakers were not the right gear for this trek. The rocks and twigs that littered the forest floor proved difficult to navigate in the unsupportive footwear. My legs ached from the climb and my head continued to throb.

As the sun set, it left the sky pale blue, the horizon streaked with red and purple and pink.

Mujada stopped in a small clearing and put her hands together in the prayer position, leaned her cheek against them, and closed her eyes. This was where we'd sleep.

I peered into the shadows, hoping to see a lean-to or some kind of structure, but there was nothing. Just the ground covered in pine needles and crisscrossed with tree roots.

We ate another MRE as darkness fell.

Mujada had blankets for both of us. I used mine like a taco, lying on one side and pulling the other over myself. Blue settled next to me, our backs lined up, each covering one side of our joint body.

The forest was quieter at night. Unlike the jungle of Costa Rica where the bugs and the birds seemed to become energized and excited by the darkness, here the forest slept as well.

Mujada lay across from me, her gun within arm's reach, just like mine. She didn't take down her hair or even loosen the laces of her boots. This was a woman who was ready. But ready for what?

Blue woke me with a wet nose to my ear. Dew coated my blanket, a layer of crystals on the dull, gray wool. Mujada continued to sleep, cradling her gun as other women would their child.

I sat up and stretched. Blue moved off to do his morning business. Did Mujada have coffee? I pulled out water and drank deeply.

The sky was dusty blue and birds sang. Pale-yellow sunlight filtered through the trees. I took a deep breath: a mix of pine and the sweetness of decay. It was beautiful. A surge of gratitude rumbled through me, that Blue and I were alive and in this place, safe in this moment.

When did I learn that? To be grateful?

Blue returned to my side and rolled onto his back. I scratched his chest.

Mujada's face was relaxed in sleep. Without the scowl of concentration wrinkling her brow, she looked young. Mujada was taller and broader than me, but couldn't be much more than twenty-one.

Strands of hair had escaped her tight bun and the morning moisture curled the wisps, creating a halo around her face.

Her eyelids fluttered, tension pulled her mouth into a frown, and her fingers tightened on the rifle. A low, keening sound emanated from her chest. It reminded me of a puppy, a lost, young thing.

Mujada's eyes popped open and she sat up quickly, her gaze unfocused, as if she was seeing the dream in front of her instead of the forest. She sucked in a shuddering breath and blinked, her eyes finding me and Blue, understanding blooming in her gaze; she was here, not there.

I wanted to comfort her but sensed that my sympathy was not welcome. Fear and loneliness are badges of courage, the burdens that warriors must carry.

Mujada turned away from me and pushed her blankets to the side, grabbing for her pack.

It was another full day of hiking before we reached our destination.

We arrived at dinnertime. Blue's nose pulsed at the scent of cooking food a mile before I picked up the smell. There were about twenty-five women sitting in a grassy field at the top of a hill. Large boulders were scattered around the open space. Women lounged against them and used them as tables.

The tall pines rose up around the tranquil meadow. The sky above was turning royal blue. As we stepped into the clearing, the chatter of voices quieted and all attention turned to us, then shifted to one woman.

She sat with three others on a rock at the center of the clearing, a plate cradled on her crossed legs. She was about my age with jet-black hair pulled back from her face. Her eyes were large and deep brown, framed by long lashes.

The woman put her plate aside and stood, her lips a straight line, eyes examining me and then shifting to Blue, and finally to Mujada.

Mujada nodded, a small tip of her chin. The woman approached and Blue's hackles rose.

There was scarring on the woman's neck—four, thick, white lines rose from her flesh—it looked like a giant paw had clawed at her throat.

I recognized her from the posters in the dining hall; this was the Tigress.

EK

She was dressed like all the women in the clearing: cargo pants tucked into combat boots and a button-down shirt ballooning out, hiding her shape. Her clothing was the same green as the trees, a slightly darker shade than the grass she crossed to greet me.

She extended her hand and I shook it—her grip was strong and her hand calloused.

"Hi." My voice was a croak. I hadn't used it for most of the day and my throat was dry from the long hike.

"Hello," she responded. "You are very welcome to be here."

"That's nice to hear. I would have preferred an invitation rather than an abduction."

She cocked her head. "I'm sorry," she looked at Mujada. "It was supposed to be an invitation."

"Probably makes more sense to send someone who speaks the same language if you're trying to invite someone to a party or whatever this is."

She laughed, leaning her head back and exposing the scars to the hazy light of dusk.

"Mujada is one of my best fighters. She has the most experience in protection and had the connections to get close to you."

"Well, she gave me a head injury."

The Tigress's smile faded, her expression turning stern as she focused on Mujada. An irrational stab of guilt lanced through me.

The Tigress spoke in a low voice and Mujada blushed before muttering a reply.

"I'm very sorry, as is Mujada," the Tigress said. "It was never my intention that you would be injured.

"So what am I doing here?"

"You're here to have dinner."

"It's a long way for a meal. I don't like to play games."

The woman smiled. "This is no game. But please, sit with me. We shall discuss the business at hand."

"Let's start with your name."

"Of course. I am Zerzan Khani."

"You prefer that to the Tigress."

She smiled and shook her head. "That is not a name I gave myself but I am proud to wear it."

"I think it suits you."

She reached up to the scars on her neck running her fingers over them, tilting her head slightly so that I could see them better. "It was a man, not an animal, that did this."

"A beast."

"Yes, I see you know by experience." She eyed the scars on my face.

"Yes, I know what humans are capable of."

"Men mostly, no?"

"I've left scars in my wake. I won't pin the violence of our species onto men alone."

She nodded. "Please, come and sit with me." She waved to a woman who dashed into the woods, returning a few minutes later with a plate of food, steam rising off it.

The Tigress seated me next to her on a rock in the center of the field, where all the other women could see us. It felt at once like an intimate dinner and a stage performance.

"Why am I here?" I asked again.

The Tigress ignored me for a moment, speaking to another woman nearby who went to Mujada and retrieved Blue's bowl and his kibble. Nice touch. "You're quite the hostess."

Zerzan smiled. "You are a very honored guest."

"I don't even know where I am."

"In a way, nobody does. This territory is claimed by three groups. The rightful owners, us, the Kurds." She held up a finger. "Daesh." A second finger. "The Iraqi government." A third finger.

"But no matter who owns it, it's still in the same location on the map. And I don't know where that is."

Zerzan brought her hand down and rubbed it against her leg. "I can show you a map if that will make you feel more comfortable. But it is our land. Kurdish land." She looked around at the women in the clearing. They watched us, their food forgotten. "The men who run the Iraqi government and those in Daesh do not respect the equality of women. But Kurdish men, they are strong and intelligent and recognize our power, purpose, and place in this world, by their side."

"Don't see many of those men around here."

She smiled. "It is easier for us to work alone. We are more terrifying. Daesh fighters are afraid to die at our hands."

"Sounds like they have some sense of your power."

"Perhaps." She smiled. "That is why they fight so hard to oppress women. Because they are afraid of us. You know, it is a part of their belief system that if a woman kills them, they don't get to go to Heaven." Zerzan's eyes lit up. "I have enjoyed sending many of them to Hell."

Blue finished his kibble and came to sit by my side. My plate of food remained untouched in front of me. "Please, eat."

It was a stew, a fragrant mix of meats and vegetables. I took a bite; it was delicious. As I ate, Zerzan spoke to a young woman who left and returned moments later with a cup made of horn and a plastic water jug filled with amber-colored liquid. She handed them to Zerzan, smiled and blushed, then hurried back to where she'd been sitting.

She was young. They were all young.

Zerzan unscrewed the cap and poured. The hoppy scent of beer wafted toward me as she passed me the cup. "Thank you. How old are these girls?"

"You must be eighteen to join our ranks. You can have no husband or children. This life must be the only life for you."

"I get that."

"But you do not have similar regulations for Joyful Justice?"

"We let those who want to fight, fight."

"It is different, our struggles."

I sipped beer and nodded. "Yes, but also the same."

"That is why I have brought you here."

"You mean invited me here?"

The Tigress smiled. "Yes, English is my second language, I apologize."

Her accent was there, making her English more lyrical and beautiful, but her grasp of the language was obviously very good. Perhaps she'd studied abroad.

"Are you enjoying the food?"

My plate was almost empty. "It was delicious. And now dinner is over so..."

"We shall have tea."

I sat back and finished off the last of my beer. Blue lay down with a sigh. The sun had set behind the mountain. The sky above was turning black, stars popping against the dark backdrop.

Tea arrived, honey brown and served in small, glass cups. We let them sit in front of us, allowing the liquid to cool.

"It is with some trepidation that I broach this subject with you."

"I don't see why. After all, you've already kidnapped me and dragged me out to the middle of nowhere, so what could your words do that your actions haven't already."

Zerzan frowned. "I wish for us to be friends."

"Hell of a beginning of a friendship."

"I apologize again."

"Look, Zerzan." I leaned forward, the perfume from the fragrant tea wafting up toward me: mint and tobacco. "I understand that you are fighting for more than just your lives here. That you're fighting for a way of life, for women, for, well, what aren't you fighting for? I want to hear what you have to say. So spit it the fuck out."

"I want you. I want to form an alliance."

Well, didn't everyone want an alliance these days? "In what way?"

"You have influence with the US government."

"Influence?" I smiled. "I wouldn't call it that. They want me to figure out how to get more women around the world to rise up and fight against Daesh. To create the kind of campaign Daesh has created that draws young men from around the globe to fight. They want me to do the same for women."

"How?"

"How did you get these women to be here?"

"These women are my family. We are from the same place. We're fighting for our land and for our people's future. There are many women like us in FKP."

"Don't you think that your fight is in the interest of everyone on the planet? That Daesh must be defeated? That their type of radicalism, their zealotry, and insanity must be wiped out?"

"Of course I do."

"But it's not just Daesh; it's not only those young men who seek to enslave women and perpetrate violence across the globe. It is everywhere. Your fight is every woman's fight."

Zerzan leaned toward me. "We need your help. Weapons, training, troops."

"The American government has refused you these things?"

"They have given us some. They have also listed us as a terrorist organization." She gestured to a machine gun that rested against the rock we sat on. "We have some weapons and we've had some training, but not the right kind."

"What do you mean, not the right kind?"

"Men have trained us, which has helped. But we are not men. And we do not fight like men." Zerzan picked up her tea and took a sip. "When we fight for our rights, we ask to be the same as men." She put the cup down. "We are not the same and so we must recognize that. We are no better or worse, but different. As a Christian is different from a Muslim is different from a Buddhist. All equal. All different. So when a man trains us, he trains us to fight like men. What we need is to fight like women."

"From what I understand, fighting like a man has worked for you so far."

"I have ended many lives. But I am only one woman and there must be tens of thousands of us, well-trained and well-equipped, in order for us to win. There are tens of thousands of them. There are more women on the planet, and yet we are subjugated to men almost everywhere. Even in your birth nation, a land of freedom, women are not equals. No law can make us equal, no decree by a man can free us from oppression. We must rise up. We must feel in our bones and know in our souls that we are equal."

"I was trained by a man. I think that I fight like a woman because I am a woman," I said.

"You are Sydney Rye. You are a great warrior. You cannot be defeated."

"That is propaganda. The same could be said about you. So what makes you think that I can do something you cannot?"

A walkie-talkie on Zerzan's hip crackled and she picked up, responding in Kurdish.

The soldiers moved quickly—one moment they were sitting around, leaning against rocks, but with one gesture from their leader, they were in action. Quietly and gracefully, the women picked up their rifles and faded into the shadows of the forest, leaving only the imprints of their bodies in the grass.

CHAPTER SIX

The Tigress took my hand; hers was the same size as mine, callouses in all the right places. The link between us was childish, like two little girls running into the woods to play rather than experienced killers lighting into the darkness to prey.

I didn't know where or who our enemy was—it could be Daesh, U.S troops sent to rescue me, or another combatant I didn't even know existed—but I believed that the Tigress and I were on the same side.

The darkness was thick with branches and the ground uneven. Blue tapped his nose to my hip, letting me know he was there. The soft sound of pine needles crinkling underfoot revealed the other bodies moving through the forest.

I stumbled over a tree root. Zerzan held me up but I felt my ankle twist and pain shoot up my leg.

Blue nudged my hip, encouraging me to continue, and I limped forward. The pain anchored me; I was here—it didn't matter specifically where on the globe—I was in this world and even without details, I knew who and what I was about.

Zerzan stopped, releasing me but staying close, a shadowed silhouette against a background of black on black. Blue brushed my hand with his nose as he turned around, scanning the forest behind us.

"Do you hear it?" Zerzan asked.

The hooting of an owl echoed and the wind wrestled with the trees. Zerzan inhaled, my ankle thrummed, and the low throb of thunder radiated. *What was real?*

Clouds parted and the white light of the moon glimmered through the trees. A cold wind raised goosebumps on my arms.

Blue was watching me, his eyes reflective green. He licked his lips and moved his feet ever so slightly.

"Who are we hiding from?"

Zerzan smiled slowly, her teeth white in the darkness.

"We are not hiding, Sydney; we are about to attack."

Blue's ears perked forward. I raised my rifle in line with him.

Zerzan, her weapon up, moved off, Blue and I in her wake.

Putting weight on my ankle sent lightning bolts shooting across my vision.

I saw them just as Blue touched my hip—dark figures crouched low, their shoulders bunched and rifles raised, moving perpendicular to us, headed for the meadow.

I took long, slow, deep breaths and blocked out the pain from my ankle.

Zerzan held her breath and fired. Flames exploded from the barrel of her rifle, lighting up her face—one eye closed as she pressed against the scope, her mouth pursed, almost as if she was offering a kiss.

The bang ricocheted through the woods and birds exploded from the trees.

One of the figures fell and the rest turned in our direction.

I dropped to the ground, Blue diving next to me.

Bullets whizzed above us, sinking into the trunks and exploding off the branches of the trees. The sticky scent of pine warred with the acrid stench of gun smoke.

Zerzan remained standing, debris zinging around her.

She fired again, the bang of her rifle the loudest in the chorus. Another figure dropped, this one accompanied by a gurgling scream.

The three remaining combatants backed away.

Zerzan showed no fear; she shot again, the backfire jerking her shoulder slightly, and another fell. The two remaining assailants turned and ran into the night. Zerzan took off after them in a sprint, her black hair reflecting the moonlight in blue streaks.

They all blurred into the darkness.

Gray smoke floated above us, picking up the light of the moon and dancing it in. The pine needles pricked through my clothing. Footsteps pounded over the soft earth. Gunshots fired.

A dark figure approached us and Blue's tail swept through the pine needles letting me know it was someone he knew. "Sydney."

I didn't recognize the whispering voice immediately, but knew that it wasn't Zerzan.

The woman moved through the woods, her rifle up, voice low but clear.

"Sydney!"

Her accent was American. It was Mary. So this was some kind of rescue mission.

I looked over at Blue who was following Mary's progress. It seemed rude not to say hello. I doubted she would come all this way just to kill me.

I whistled and Mary stopped, turning slowly toward us, her rifle moving with her gaze. I waved at her as her eyes scanned over me.

Mary crouched next to us. "Don't worry; we are going to get you out of here."

"How did you find me?"

"We tracked the transport truck that Mujada stole. Then located you using drone surveillance."

"Nifty."

"What?"

Blue tensed next to me at the sound of approaching footfalls.

I shook my head and held a finger to my lips then shifted in the direction of the sound.

It was strange to feel that I had no enemies. There was the Tigress and her soldiers who wanted to keep me with them versus Mary and her men who wanted to take me away. Neither side wanted to hurt me: both believed that I had value.

Enough value that they would die for me. Why weren't they on the same side?

EK

"This is going to sound crazy," I said to Mary. "But I think we are all on the same side here."

"They kidnapped you."

"Yeah, but only because they want the same things as you."

Mary's rifle was raised and aimed at the approaching figures.

How could she know if they were her friends or enemies in this darkness? Perhaps she'd brought all men in order to keep it straight.

I started to stand up, but Mary grabbed my arm. "What are you doing?" Her voice was harsh and worried.

"Brokering a peace accord."

It sounded crazy but it made sense.

Everyone was on the same side. The enemy—Daesh—wasn't here. By killing each other, we were winning the war for them.

I pulled free of Mary and stood, being careful not to put too much weight on my twisted ankle. The dark shapes in front of me stopped and braced themselves, rifles aimed at me. "I'm Sydney Rye!"

They lowered their weapons—they didn't want to kill me. That was the first agreement we could come to.

I waved them over. As the three women approached, I saw that they were the Tigress's soldiers. They appeared older than they had in the meadow at sunset, the moonlight highlighting the fierce determination in their expressions.

"Mary, I want you to meet the Tiger Cubs."

"What?"

"Remember the Tigress, the woman who Daesh claimed to have killed, cutting off her head, blah, blah, blah?"

Mary nodded.

"Well, this was her party you just broke up. These are her soldiers." I pointed at the rifles they held. "You gave them those guns. Well, obviously not you. But they were supplied by the US government. It's kind of like you guys have the same boss. Except you don't listen to your boss." I looked over at Mary. She didn't respond. "And these ladies, they listen to their boss but their boss doesn't listen to you."

"Are you drunk?" Mary asked in a low voice. "Because you're sounding kind of drunk."

"I had like half a beer. But I really don't think that's what's making me talk like this. I think it's that the situation is so truly ridiculous it's actually difficult not to laugh. But if you all could stop shooting each other, I think we could sit down and have a conversation."

The soldiers were eyeing Mary. She was eyeing them back.

"Any of you have a radio?" I asked the women in front of me. They didn't respond and I turned to Mary who translated. One of them stepped forward and held out a walkie-talkie. "Can we get Zerzan on this thing?"

Mary translated and the woman nodded, opening a channel and speaking into the radio. The response crackled, sounding very loud and foreign in the dark forest. The woman handed me the walkie-talkie "Zerzan?"

"I am here, Sydney."

"Let's stop killing each other. I think we're on the same team here. How about we meet back at the meadow and I talk to all of you."

"These men attacked us. They are dangerous to my soldiers; I cannot let them live."

"You said you wanted my help, now you're getting it. Tell your troops to stand down." I raised my chin at Mary, signaling that she should do the same. Mary held my gaze as she raised her wrist to her mouth and spoke into her sleeve.

Obviously Mary had newer technology; there was no crackle, no pop, which was much safer in these conditions.

The exact kind of stuff that the Tigress and her team needed.

"Zerzan, they are standing down and now you tell your troops do the same. I promise you, I'll help you win this thing."

Walkie-talkies crackled throughout the forest.

"Let's head back to the meadow ladies." I started to walk and Blue touched my hip. I looked at him and he turned around—I was walking in the wrong direction. I laughed because it was just too funny.

Mary and the Tiger cubs eyed me warily; did they think I was crazy?

Mary shook her head. Was she regretting her decision to deal with me?

EK

My ankle was throbbing, but I ignored it as I returned to the rock in the center of the meadow. Blue stood by my side. I gestured for Mary to sit next to me.

The three Tiger Cubs stood around us, their rifles lowered but ready. Mary radioed our location to her team, and slowly the clearing filled with bodies.

Both sides had lost people, which was going to make it harder for them to come together. However, since we all shared a goal of defeating Daesh, there was hope.

Zerzan approached slowly, her gun aimed at the sky; her eyes narrowed as she scanned the group of soldiers on Mary's side of the meadow.

Seven men stood behind Mary. They wore black fatigues, body armor, and helmets. Night vision goggles covered their eyes. They looked more like monsters than men; some kind of science fiction machine soldier sent here from outer space.

The animosity radiating off the female fighters was palpable; these creatures had arrived on their turf and tried to take what was theirs, killing in the process.

"Zerzan, I'd like you to meet Mary." The two women eyed each other, but neither extended their hand. "I think you have more in common than you realize, and I believe that together we can create a powerful alliance."

"So they didn't kidnap you?" Mary asked.

"No, I got kidnapped." I looked over at Blue and he turned away; was he ashamed he let me get abducted?

"So?" Mary left the word hanging in the air.

"You both want the same thing: to defeat Daesh. Both of you want to use the powerful fear that women strike into their hearts to do it. And both of you seem to think that I can help. So I suggest you let me." I addressed Zerzan. "You need support, weapons, technology. Look at those men. They are covered in all the things that you need."

"And yet I still managed to kill several of them."

The men bristled. Mary turned to look at them, giving a small shake of her head.

"Yes," I said. "You did kill them and that's because you have superior knowledge of this place. I don't even know where we are." Turning to Mary I asked, "Do you know where we are?"

"Of course."

"How can you? This is disputed territory. You might be able to find it on the map, but that alone would not give you knowledge of this place. There is a history here and there is a war that is being waged which has nothing to do with America. These women, Kurdish fighters, have been trying to hold this land on behalf of their people."

"We have been holding it. There is no trying about it."

I nodded, acknowledging Zerzan's interruption. "Right, and they will continue to control this land with or without American help, but if we want to take land back from Daesh, to go on the offensive and help to rid the planet of Daesh, then you have to work together."

"How can we trust her?" Mary asked.

"I have the same question," Zerzan said. "All of the promises that America makes are broken."

"This is going to be different. This isn't a promise between FKP and the USA. It's a promise made between Zerzan and Mary. This is going to be completely and totally personal."

Mary and Zerzan stopped glaring at each other and stared at me.

"Are you afraid to give your word? Are you afraid that you don't have the power to back it up?"

"I am afraid of nothing." Zerzan straightened her spine and narrowed her eyes at me. "But she is not a leader. She is just another soldier working for the US government."

"That's not entirely true. She has lots of discretion. The US government would never officially work with me. I'm on the most wanted list in several countries and I'm a known leader of a terrorist organization. Yet, she is here, trying to get me back from you."

"I do have discretion," Mary agreed. "I'm just not sure I'd want to use it in order to form an alliance with her."

"Don't be a dumbass, Mary. You want to attract women to this fight, then you're going to need Zerzan." I gestured to the other women in the meadow. "This is what will get women from all over the world to leave their homes and come here to fight: the promise of power and strength and equality. Why do men flock to Daesh?"

"Disenfranchised Muslim men are angry and easily turned into jihadists. Zerzan and her followers are nationalists, fighting for their homeland. Whereas women without such an obvious stake are not as easily convinced that violence is the answer," Mary answered.

"Why can't we go after every young woman who is online right now posting memes about how we don't get paid enough? We'd only need a small fraction of them to actually get on a plane and come here to fight."

"You're the one who said that was near impossible," Mary reminded me.

"That was before I met Zerzan and saw what she has going here." *Before my most recent head injury.*

"But how can we trust them?" Mary asked.

"How can I trust you?" Zerzan replied.

"You killed five of my men," Mary spat.

"You attacked us." Zerzan's voice was low, but dangerous.

"You fired first."

The two leaders stood across from each other, their bodies tense, necks extended, hands clenched on their rifles. The troops on both sides followed their leaders' subtle cues and fingers migrated toward triggers. Blue's hackles were rising.

I forced myself to remain seated despite every instinct in my body telling me to stand and prepare to fight.

"Calm down, both of you."

Zerzan and Mary continued to stare at each other. I spoke again, careful to keep my voice even. "I am asking you both to take a step back and a deep breath. Please."

Mary's gaze flicked to me and then she stepped back, daring Zerzan to do the same with a glare. They each sucked in a big breath and then let it out slowly, maintaining eye contact with each other.

I knew that we were on the verge of something; whether it would be bloodshed or a handshake, I wasn't sure. But there wasn't much time before the decision was made.

"What would you need, Mary, in order to make this work?"

Mary glanced at me and I could see that she was thinking. Trying to change the track of her mind from one of aggression to one of negotiation. "Zerzan, what about you?" I went on. "What would you need?"

"Intelligence, weapons, air support, supplies like food, and technology. I like those helmets," she said pointing at the men behind Mary. "You have to be a very good shot to kill one of those men, and most Daesh fighters are not very good shots."

"Mary?"

"I'd probably be able to provide those things, but what do we do about the men she killed?" Mary kept her voice low. "We can't work with a woman who has killed American soldiers."

Unsure how to proceed, I took a deep breath, letting it out slowly, allowing my mind to turn over the problem: Mary was being a pain in the ass and Zerzan was born a pain in the ass. Both were conditioned by their experiences to act this way.

I understood perfectly, because I was the same. There was a key here, something that would let them both be satisfied and work together. I just wasn't entirely sure what it was.

Blue touched his nose to my hand where it rested on the rock. I looked over at him and held his gaze for a moment, pulling strength from his calm demeanor.

"I understand that the men who were shot must be recognized—"

"It is traditional for them to be avenged," Mary interrupted me.

"Well, tradition is not what we are going for here. We want revolution, no? You want women to rise up and defend not only what is theirs, but what could be theirs."

"This land is ours," Zerzan said, her voice strong and clear. "The US government believes that it belongs to the Iraqi government. They do not recognize our sovereignty."

"Maybe you have to make them," Mary said.

"How?" Zerzan raised her eyebrows.

"If you help to exterminate Daesh—wage a propaganda war as powerful as theirs—then the American government would have no choice but to recognize your power and your rights."

"We can do this. With your help."

"What about the men who died here? We can't forget them."

"We can make them martyrs," Zerzan suggested.

"What do you mean?"

"We shall honor them. They died to bring us together. So we shall honor them. They shall become martyrs and forever be remembered and praised."

The sound of approaching drones was quiet, barely a whisper really. Blue noticed it first, standing and tapping his nose against my leg, then directing my attention to the sky.

It was one of Mary's soldiers who stated what was becoming quickly obvious to everyone in the meadow. "Incoming!"

Drones whizzed above us, almost impossible to see except for when they passed before the moon, throwing a flicker of shadow onto our gathering.

A low whistle pierced the air. I tipped off the rock and flattened my body next to it, my arms around Blue. Mary yelled into her sleeve. Zerzan stood still, her face turned upward.

An explosion hit outside of the meadow, tearing trees from the ground and flinging them through the air, an orange fire raging after them.

Before the smoke could reach us, another shell hit on the far side of my rock. A hot wind rushed across the meadow, leveling the grass, followed by shrapnel and clumps of dirt raining down. Screaming sounded into the night as a man's soul was wrenched from his body.

A third shell landed, launching trees into the sky, their branches becoming projectiles.

Black smoke filled the air along with moaning and crying. I released Blue, who shook himself. I slowly stood, using the rock to return to my feet.

The meadow was transformed. Where there had been gentle moonlight, there was now hungry flames. Where soldiers had stood, now bodies lay.

Zerzan was on her knees next to one of her women. She was holding the soldier's hand and caressing her forehead.

The woman lifted her head and looked down her body. Her legs were gone and blood pooled around her bottom half. There was no sign of the limbs she had lost. The soldier lowered her head to the ground and looked up at Zerzan.

Her body, which had been rigid with fear and pain, relaxed into death.

Zerzan stood, her hair free from its ponytail dancing in the wind as smoke swirled around her. The Tigress's face was a mask, a sculpture of calmness; she appeared neither surprised nor distraught.

Blue tapped my hip again and began to move to our left, where the fire had not yet reached.

The pine needles were perfect fuel and the trees around us were exploding with flames. We had to get out of there if we wanted to live. I scanned the ground, trying to see if there was anyone I could help, anyone who could move enough for me to hobble out with them. Mary was sitting on the other side of the rock, her back leaning against the stone.

Blue whined and then barked, looking at our escape path, encouraging me to leave. I crouched next to Mary and saw a piece of a tree limb had pierced her shoulder.

Blood soaked her shirt. Her face was pale, eyes glazed.

"Mary!" I yelled to be heard over the fire which was consuming the forest around us in loud bangs and pops.

Mary was looking past me and I followed her gaze. Her soldiers were dead, sprawled around the meadow, many of them missing limbs, their bodies on fire. The scent of burning flesh and plastic was thick in the air.

"We have to go." I reached around her, getting my hands behind her back so that I could lift her. She shook her head. "I don't have time to argue with you." I pulled her against me and shifted her body so that her stomach was at my shoulder. I stood, with her draped over me and ran for the tree line without looking back at the carnage.

Blue led the way, running in front of me, his tail high and white, making it easy to see.

The underbrush grabbed at my legs and smoke burned my lungs. My only goal was to escape the flames. Mary groaned.

My injured ankle made my pace slow and halting.

Blue kept barking his encouragement. I coughed, choking on the smoke.

The heat of the fire was intense. Sweat dripped into my eyes, down my spine, and pooled between Mary and me.

She stopped groaning and her body went slack, getting even heavier.

I hoped she'd passed out from the pain, but worried that I was risking my life to carry a corpse through the woods.

I dropped to my knees on the pine needles. Blue barked at me, insistent that we needed to keep moving.

Mary's eyes were open and unseeing. What I had thought was sweat was blood. My shirt was soaked, and Mary was dead. Beyond her shoulder injury, a chunk of rock had hit her thigh, severing her femoral artery.

I found the comm unit in her sleeve and pulled it free, shoving it into my pocket.

I patted her down and found a handgun at her hip ,which I also took. I glanced back toward the meadow; there was a wall of fire behind me.

What had happened to Zerzan?

She was too much of a survivor to die with her soldiers. She was not the type of woman who would allow grief to take her down. I stood again and Blue barked more insistently, warning that time was limited, reminding me that fires could move faster than you thought.

I glanced down at Mary once more before following Blue deeper into the woods.

EK

Blue led me away from the flames, and after an hour, we reached a stream. He ran into the water and lapped at it.

I contemplated drinking the water myself but couldn't risk a parasite. I did wade into the rushing stream, washing myself and my blood-soaked clothing.

The water smelled fresh and green but the scent of burning flesh and plastic remained in my nose. The fire glowed on the horizon. I hadn't seen a road or any sign of humans.

What happened to Mujada? She wasn't in the meadow. I had not seen her since she left us at dinner.

Could Blue lead me back to the road and the transport vehicle? We hadn't passed this stream on our hike in, so some kind of change of direction was required.

I was shivering in my wet shirt and Blue came and sat next to me, leaning his big, warm, wet body against my side.

I debated whether to continue or rest here for the night. Blue stood and nudged my shoulder, implying that we should go on.

I followed him along the bank of the stream. Mary's comm unit made a sound and I pushed the earpiece into my ear. "Come in, Blue Eagle, come in, Blue Eagle."

I thought I recognized Declan's voice but wasn't entirely sure. Should I respond? Blue forged ahead, his wet paws picking up dirt and pine needles as we progressed.

I moved slower as the pain in my ankle developed into an almost unbearable throb.

The voice in my ear continued to page Blue Eagle until, exhausted and in pain, my throat dry from smoke and thirst, I decided to risk a response.

"This is Sydney Rye."

"Sydney?"

"That's right," I croaked, my voice breaking under the strain of thirst and smoke inhalation.

"What the fuck happened?"

"Somebody bombed us."

"Where is Blue Eagle?"

"Mary?" There was a pause and then an affirmative response. "She's dead."

"Where are you now?"

I laughed and looked around at the dark forest, the babbling brook and Blue sitting next to me, his tongue lolling out of his head, his tail twitching back and forth.

"I don't know. I haven't known for quite some time."

"Can you give us any detailed information about your location?"

I sat down, the pain in my ankle too much to continue on, and closed my eyes. At least my shirt had dried a little, but I was still freezing cold.

Blue moved behind me, providing both warmth and physical support.

"Let me sleep on it." I pulled the earpiece out before his response.

Curled up on the bank of the stream, Blue at my back, our spines lined up, Mary's handgun next to me, I fell asleep.

EK

Blue woke me with a growl. He was standing, looking over me. The sky above us was still black, but a touch of light grayed the horizon behind Blue.

I followed his gaze, looking in what I now knew to be west, and saw that the fire was still burning, a soft, orange glow at the very edge of what we could see.

Blue growled again and I heard a person moving through the forest. I put my finger on the pistol's trigger and lay still.

"Blue, down."

He lowered himself slowly, resting his head on my hip so that he could stare past me. The person came into view, her form outlined by the orange light from the fire. Long hair created a halo around her head. Zerzan. She moved with a fearless concentration, following the path that Blue and I had taken along the stream's edge.

She paused and crouched down to examine the ground, the muzzle of her rifle silhouetted against the light behind her. She stood and continued toward us.

I sat up slowly. She stopped her approach and raised her weapon. Did she plan to kill me? Maybe she thought I betrayed her. But that would be very shallow thinking. She was smarter than that.

"Zerzan, it's me, Sydney." I kept my pistol aimed at her, but held it low, in the shadows, where she could not see it.

Zerzan lowered her rifle. "Are you hurt?"

"Nothing serious."

She closed the space between us.

"Are you okay?" I asked.

"I just lost twenty of my sisters, I am not okay. But I am alive."

"I'm sorry for your loss." She nodded but didn't make eye contact. "Do you have any water?"

Zerzan pulled a backpack around, opening it and retrieving a plastic bottle of water. She passed it to me and I drank.

"Why did that happen?" I asked.

Zerzan's lip twitched into a small smile and she shook her head. "This is war. Things like that happen all the time."

"All the time? Who was it? How did they find us?"

"They may have been watching your friends."

"My friends? Mary wasn't my friend; she was blackmailing me."

"What do you mean?"

"She wanted the same thing you wanted, and you used similar means. Both of you wanted my help, both of you were willing to use force to get it." *Karma's a bitch.*

"I'm sorry."

I caught Zerzan's eyes in the dusty light of dawn and she reached out and took my hand. Her skin was warm and rough. She smelled like fire and smoke. "I would like us to be real friends. I don't want to force you to do anything."

"I want to help. For a moment there, I thought I was going to succeed. But then the world blew up." I shook my head and looked down at our joined hands.

"There are lots of ways to help. I think that we can still make something good happen. I am still alive, and so are you. What Mary wanted, others must want as well. We will continue with our plan."

Zerzan shared her food with me and then we headed in the direction Blue and I had been walking. Our progress was slow because of my ankle, but Zerzan didn't complain. The day brightened and warmed and my clothing was finally dry, though the chill in my bones did not relent.

We did not speak much, preserving our strength for the trek. It was late afternoon when we arrived back at the road where Mujada had left the transport vehicle. I saw it through the trees just as Zerzan took my arm to stop me. She motioned for Blue and me to stay and then circled around, checking the area to make sure it was secure.

I sat down but kept Mary's pistol in my hand. Zerzan returned and helped me up. When we got to the truck, she assisted me into the passenger seat. Blue jumped up into the foot well, being careful of my ankle.

The communication device that I'd been ignoring for the past twelve hours started to make noise again. I put it into my ear thinking that if Zerzan and I were going to make a deal with the devil, then we'd have to talk to him. I was surprised to hear Dan's voice in my ear. "Sydney, come in, Sydney."

"Dan?"

"Thank God. Sydney, I have been trying to reach you for hours. Are you okay?"

"Yeah, I'm fine."

Zerzan climbed into the driver's seat and turned on the truck. Its big, diesel engine rumbled.

"What's going on?" Dan asked. "I wasn't sure what happened to you. I've been following your beacon and I know you've been moving slowly. Where are you hurt?"

I couldn't help but smile. "I sprained my ankle. Sneakers are not the best for long hikes in the woods."

Zerzan backed up and turned the truck around.

"Well you're in some really fucked up territory right now."

"Yeah, but I'm on the move. Just got into a truck."

"How can I help?"

"Right now, I think I've got everything under control." Zerzan looked over at me raising her eyebrows at the suggestion that everything was *under control*. "We got attacked last night. Bombed."

"It was the Russians."

"I'm not going to ask how you know that."

"I don't think I have time to explain it to you. Where are you headed now?"

"We're going to a doctor so I can get my ankle looked at and then I'm going to try and negotiate an alliance between the Kurdish female fighters and the US government."

There was silence on the other end for so long that I wondered if we'd been disconnected but then finally Dan replied. "Okay."

I laughed "What? That doesn't sound like my area of expertise?"

"No, it's not that. I'm just surprised you're realizing it. I think it's great. Let me know what we can do."

"I will."

"I'll be in touch again, check in on you."

Dan got off the line and was immediately replaced by Declan's voice. "Come in, Red Eagle, come in, Red Eagle."

"Are you calling me Red Eagle?" I asked.

"Yes. Please return to base as soon as possible. Or we can come and get you."

"I'll be in touch tomorrow to set something up. I think you'll like what I have to offer you."

I took the comm out of my ear and looked over at Zerzan. She was concentrating on the road. It was narrow and bumpy.

"How long until we get to where we are going?"

"My village is close. I have not been home in a very long time. But we have to get that ankle looked at. And I have none of my supplies. They were all lost."

I watched her face, looking for some kind of emotion, grief over the loss of her soldiers, trepidation at returning home, but her gaze stayed steady on the road, her hands relaxed on the wheel, and her expression one of grim determination. She hardly seemed human. Could she be for real? I shivered as fear prickled along my spine. Could she be a figment of my imagination?

CHAPTER SEVEN

Tears welled in Zerzan's father's eyes as he held her tight to his chest. Taller than Zerzan by a few inches, he kissed the top of her head while speaking words I did not understand, though the sentiment was clear. Her mother's face was wet with tears and her hands shook as she embraced her daughter.

I could see the family resemblance; Zerzan had her father's nose, straight and narrow, and her mother's large, almond-shaped eyes. Four younger siblings—two boys and two girls—hugged Zerzan and all spoke at once, their voices rising as they clamored to be heard.

Zerzan's expression remained calm and her eyes dry. How could she be so unaffected? My eyes stung and it wasn't even my elated family.

Witnessing such unbridled love, such a welcome homecoming, was special and I at once envied and feared for Zerzan. She had so much to lose.

This is what Zerzan was fighting for, what all her soldiers died defending. Those women's families would never get to welcome them home. My throat tightened and I swallowed to clear it.

Neighbors came out of their houses. Young mothers held babies in their arms, others had toddlers on their hips, older children holding onto their legs. Elderly women helped with the kids, bending over to hold tiny hands. Older men, hunched with age, black hair turned bright silver, stood with the women and children.

There were no young men.

This was what war left behind; part of a community, but not a whole. Women like Zerzan fought to keep it safe, to make sure that they could live here in this beautiful village. But no one was truly at peace because their hearts were out there fighting; their husbands, children, and siblings.

This was why I kept my distance from people: If you loved someone, then more than your own life was forever at risk. I would rather die than lose another person I loved.

Zerzan turned to the gathered villagers, her mother still holding onto her arm and a younger sister wrapped around her waist, the girl's cheek pressed against her stomach. She glanced at me and, for a moment, I saw searing pain in her expression, but then her eyes shuttered and she spoke.

The language was beautiful, lyrical. Her voice was loud and carried to all those gathered around us. Her voice did not break, but I could see the hearts of those around us splintering. She was telling them that their daughters and their sisters were dead. I didn't need to understand the words to witness the devastation they created.

They were like the bombs that had rained down on us.

Now I realized that the rumble of the truck as we had approached the village was like the buzz of the drones that signaled the coming attack.

And Zerzan climbing out alone was like the whistling warning of the bombs.

Her words the explosion that blew all hope away.

The loss of their loved ones was the fire; it would burn bright for a length of time, then slowly smolder and finally extinguish, having consumed all that it could, leaving nothing but black soot and char.

Would their hearts stay empty or, like the forest, would new life grow from the ashes?

EK

Inside Zerzan's family home, the sunlight streamed in through clean windows, creating bright patches in the dark space. We entered into the kitchen and the smell of freshly baked bread and rich spices filled the air.

Blue stayed very close to me, but looked back at the crowd we'd left outside.

They took strength from each other but they also bled for each other.

I wanted to do something about it, to transform their suffering into rage. That's what I'd been doing for almost five years.

I took the pain of my brother's death and I made it into something else, something I could use. Anger lets you take action, fills you with burning desire.

Grief is like an anvil on your chest. It weighs you down, suffocates you, leaving you with nothing to do but bear its weight and try to survive.

Zerzan's mother turned to me and reached out a shaking hand. The lines on her face were deep grooves. Her age was hard to determine because the strain of her life had amplified the years. How many children had she borne? And how many still lived?

She reached out to me and took my arm, squeezing my bicep and giving me a smile. She said something I didn't understand but Zerzan translated.

"She is offering you food."

I smiled back at her and was about to refuse but Zerzan spoke again. "Say yes. It will make her happy if you say yes."

I nodded. "Yes, thank you. How do I say thank you?"

"Spas."

I tried to pronounce it and Zerzan's mother smiled at me, releasing my arm and patting my cheek before moving toward the stove.

One of Zerzan's sisters, a girl about twelve, was staring at Blue. "You can pet him if you want."

I gestured for Blue to sit and then beckoned the girl over. She wrung her hands before taking a tentative step in our direction.

Zerzan's father, brothers, and remaining sister moved into the next room while Zerzan stepped up to help her mom at the stove.

"What's your name?" I pointed to the girl. Touching my own chest I said, "Sydney."

I pointed at Blue and told her his name.

"Jiyan." The girl reached a hand toward Blue. He leaned into it and when her hand touched the soft fur at the top of his head, her face broke into a wide smile.

Jiyan was skinny and looked like she'd just gone through a growth spurt; her skirt ended at her calves instead of her ankles and the sleeves of her shirt stopped in the middle of her forearms. Her black hair was held back in a braid.

Sunlight from a window caught the side of her face. She said something I didn't understand and Zerzan translated for me. "She asks how old he is."

"Around six, I think. I adopted him from a shelter, so don't know for sure."

Zerzan translated and Jiyan looked up at me confused.

"She does not understand what you mean by shelter."

"In the US, when dogs have no homes, they go into shelters until someone adopts them." Zerzan translated and her sister replied.

"What happens if no one adopts them?" Zerzan asked

"It depends on the shelter." It was strange to be standing here in this cozy kitchen, surrounded by all this familial love and excitement at the reunion, yet still be able to hear the weeping of others outside, mourning the loss of their own sisters and daughters, and be talking about what happened to dogs in America that didn't get adopted.

"You can just tell her that they all get adopted."

Zerzan smiled and relayed my message. Jiyan nodded and returned her attention to Blue.

Zerzan's mother spoke and she translated. "Go sit down; we will be there in a moment."

"Can I do anything to help?"

Zerzan shook her head and said something to Jiyan. The young girl took my hand and led me into the next room. Her skin was soft, her bones small, everything about her young and new and vulnerable.

The living room was bigger than the kitchen, but still small for such a large family. Bookshelves filled with leather-bound volumes lined one wall.

Zerzan's father came down the stairs from the second floor holding a black doctor's bag. He gestured for me to have a seat in one chair that faced an empty fireplace.

My shoes and legs were caked with mud, and as I untied my laces, some of it broke off and fell onto the clean floor. "Sorry."

Her father just smiled at me. I guess when you have that many kids, a little mud on the floor isn't a huge concern.

I removed my shoe and sock, pushing up my sweatpants' leg. Zerzan's father, whose name I still didn't know, spoke to one of his sons who hurried into the other room, returning with a bowl of water and a washcloth.

I reached down so that I could wash my own leg but he shook his head and did it himself. A surge of emotion flowed, gratitude.

Zerzan came in as her father cleaned my injured ankle and examined the bruised swelling. She carried a tray and put it down on the coffee table. Her siblings each grabbed a glass of tea and one of the pastries that filled the room with a sweet and mouthwatering scent.

Zerzan stood behind her father looking down at my ankle and spoke to him. He responded. "He does not think it's broken." Zerzan's father moved my ankle up and down and I winced. "Can you move your toes?"

I nodded. "I don't think it's broken. I know what a broken bone feels like."

Zerzan smiled. "I'm sure you do. He says that he will wrap it for you and that you should stay off it for a couple of days. We can give you some pain medicine that will also help the swelling."

"Spas," I said. Jiyan giggled into her hand. "Was it my pronunciation?"

Zerzan nodded. "Nice try though."

"Where did you learn English?"

"I told you, we had American trainers. They taught me."

"It's excellent."

"I was always good at languages. My father spoke seven languages."

"Wow. And a doctor."

"No, my grandfather's the doctor." Zerzan gestured to the man who was wrapping my ankles. "My father died in the war."

"I'm sorry."

"Thank you. There are many losses." Zerzan turned away from me and picked up one of the steaming glasses of tea, passing it to me. "Should I get water for Blue?"

"Please."

Zerzan left the room again as her mother came in carrying another tray filled with food. She smiled at me and insisted I take one of the sweet breads she offered.

Another pulse of gratitude flowed through me.

I had already agreed to broker a deal with Zerzan and the US government, but as her grandfather wrapped my ankle, I knew that even if Homeland Security didn't help them, I would use the resources of Joyful Justice to make sure Zerzan got what she needed.

EK

We left Zerzan's family house as the sun set, well fed, cleaned up, and bandaged. We had agreed to go back to the base where my journey had started and to convince Declan to strike the alliance I had been trying to arrange with Mary. Zerzan had given me a clean uniform of hers. It fit almost perfectly. We really were cut from the same cloth.

By the time we'd climbed back into the transport vehicle, Jiyan and Blue were great friends. He'd spent the hour preceding our exit lying on the floor with his head in her lap as she patted his face and whispered to him.

As we drove away in the peachy-orange light of the sunset, I watched Zerzan's family in the side mirror. They waved until the road turned and I lost sight of them.

The neighbors did not come out to say goodbye. Maybe they would have, but we left quickly and as quietly as a diesel engine allows.

"When Mujada kidnapped me, was that your forces attacking?" I asked Zerzan.

"No."

"Who was it then?"

"Daesh, probably. Mujada wasn't going to wait to find out."

"Right, but the whole time we were there, Mujada seemed very nervous. Like she was expecting something to happen."

"Mujada is always expecting something to happen."

"Where is she?"

"She has her own mission."

"Will we see her again?"

"I will, depends on how long you stick around." Zerzan took her eyes off the road for a moment to hold my gaze.

"I'll be here as long as it takes."

She nodded and returned her attention to the dirt track.

I retrieved Mary's communication device from the glove compartment where I had stashed it. "I'll see if I can raise anyone on the radio, let them know we are coming."

"That's a good idea, we don't want them shooting at us."

"Oh no. Not that."

Zerzan laughed.

Turning on the unit, I immediately heard a voice asking for Red Eagle. "This is Red Eagle."

"Red Eagle. What is your location?" It was Declan's voice.

"I'm headed back to you."

"When?"

"A few hours."

"I'll see you then."

I put the device back into the glove compartment.

"Let's get very clear about what you need," I said.

"I need more fighters. I need better equipment. And I need them to stay out of my way."

"You mentioned air support before."

"Yes, that's important as well, but it is better for us to kill Daesh fighters ourselves rather than bombs. Even if a woman is flying the plane, they will have no way to know that. But when they see our faces, when they see our bodies, they will know that they are going to Hell."

Zerzan was smiling.

73

"How do you think we can attract other women besides those in your community to come and fight?"

"How does Daesh do it? We must do it better and smarter."

"And how do we do that?"

"The call to war is stronger for men because they enjoy the blood. Yes?"

"Right."

"Obviously there are women, like us, who are also drawn to war. We would be soldiers no matter what."

"I don't know, I think we both chose this route because of something that happened, something personal. Maybe that's the key. We have to figure out how to make this personal for everyone we recruit. You are fighting because you are defending your homeland. What would motivate women from other lands?"

"Why are you fighting?"

"I lost someone and fighting is the only way to keep the grief from swallowing me whole."

We were silent for a long time. The night grew pitch black, our headlights the only illumination. We came off the rough track and onto blacktop.

The tires droned, the engine was steady, and the night was still.

My admission was heavy in the air even an hour later. Zerzan knew about grief. It must have been a similar catalyst that sent her to the front lines. For women like us territory could not be the sole motivator. The safety of those we loved and revenge for those we lost was what drove us into battle.

How could we find more women like us? Women who would be willing to give their lives to send men to hell?

The Daesh fighters had a book, a religious zealotry that gave them incredible power—a god who, in their minds, sanctioned their violence.

The weapon we had against them—their own belief that dying by a woman's hand barred them from the Heaven they so desperately wished to enter—was powerful, but not inspiring.

Joyful Justice's ranks were filled with women who fought for their own freedom, their own revenge. It was all very personal. How do you make somebody else's fight personal?

I was here, sitting in this truck with a woman I'd just met, heading back to a military compound where I could very well lose my life, or my freedom, in the hope of helping her cause.

But I didn't wish this life on anyone else.

Recruiting women to come and live like this, with this ball of anger as their constant companion, wasn't noble. It was cruel.

My mother's face filled my mind's eye. The way she looked when I was young, before my father passed. When she was the happy mother of two happy kids, the wife of a man she loved.

That woman was gone. As gone as my murdered brother. She died with my father; she drowned in a bottle— April Humbolt was reborn a fire-and-brimstone preacher's wife. Her religion saved her body and destroyed our relationship.

She thought James was in Hell because he was gay. She thought her daughter, Joy, was dead...probably figured she was in hell too.

And maybe I was. Maybe this life I lived was Hell.

Another set of headlights appeared, coming toward us, and Zerzan and I both stiffened. "Who's that?" I asked.

"I have no idea."

CHAPTER EIGHT

From the height of the headlights, it was probably military. It wasn't a sedan out for an evening drive through disputed territory.

Suddenly, white heat ballooned under the vehicle and it rocketed into the air. Tires exploded off as the squat body of a Hummer was revealed in the bright light of the bomb.

Zerzan slammed on the brakes and threw the truck into park, grabbing her rifle. "Get out!"

I opened my door; Blue and I jumped out, Zerzan tumbling after us.

The Hummer landed on its side and flipped across the center of the road, finally settling on its roof in the dirt. Orange, blue, and white flames spat out of the undercarriage, reaching for the stars.

Zerzan hunkered next to the truck and I crouched beside her.

A tire wobbled down the center of the road followed by a hot rush of wind smelling of burning plastic, roasting flesh, and gasoline.

The Humvee's gas tank ignited, completely engulfing the vehicle in a thundering whoosh of flames. Chalky black smoke blossomed into the night. This was an ISIS attack and the attackers were likely still nearby.

"If they see we are women," Zerzan said. "They will try to take us rather than kill us."

"What if they blow up the truck before they see that we are women?"

"If they had the weapons for that, they would have already done it."

"Comforting."

Dark figures came down from the hills and circled around the fire. They were shouting to each other, celebrating. The valley amplified the sound so that we could hear them over the loud sputtering of the flames.

Blue touched his wet nose to my shoulder and let out a low growl. I followed his gaze toward the rear of the truck but didn't see any movement.

Zerzan whispered. "They are trying to distract us. More will come."

"I think they're here."

Blue's hackles raised and his lips pulled back from his teeth.

Zerzan raised her rifle in the direction Blue indicated.

Boots jogging on the dirt shoulder.

"Stay close," I told Blue. They might want to take women, but I was sure they would have no problem killing dogs.

"Pretend to be injured," Zerzan said.

I grabbed my ankle and let out a moan, pitching it high so that it would be clear I was a woman, one in distress.

Zerzan pressed her eye into the site of the rifle. She fired, the bang was followed by a thump as a body fell into the dirt.

With only a handgun, I had no chance of hitting moving targets in the dark at that distance.

Zerzan's weapon blasted again, twice. A yelp of pain.

Zerzan laid her rifle down and unsheathed the knife at her waist.

"What are you doing?" I whispered.

"Out of rounds."

Staying low, Zerzan moved alongside the truck. I gestured for Blue to go under the vehicle behind me where he would be hard to see, and safer from stray bullets.

Zerzan disappeared around the back of the truck and I waited, my ears straining to hear movement.

The low moans of one of Zerzan's victims echoed in the valley, making it hard to judge his distance.

Blue growled and I glanced at him. The fighters who had been celebrating by the Humvee were moving down the road toward us, still laughing and chatting with each other, their gate a slow jog.

They didn't look worried about taking out two women. I felt a smile spreading across my face. They were all going to die.

Turning back toward the rear of the truck I could make out black shapes in the darkness. I waited, saving my bullets for when I had a clear shot.

Our truck's headlights, while facing in the opposite direction, illuminated the night enough that I could make out the men's shapes and see that they each held a rifle.

From the bulk of their clothing, it appeared they were wearing bulletproof vests and so I waited another moment until the three of them were almost at the truck's back bumper before raising my gun in a smooth motion, aiming at the one in the center and firing a bullet into his face.

The man's head jerked back and a bolt of lightning zigzagged across my vision. I moved my pistol to the left and shot again. I missed.

Zerzan leapt from the back of the truck landing on the man closest to her. The one I'd missed was coming at me fast, his body hunched around his gun, making the target of his face very difficult to find so I just shot at the center of him. The bullet hit and he twisted but didn't go down, stumbling forward, almost upon me.

I fired again, this time hitting his helmet. At that close range it penetrated the metal and he fell forward and splayed at my feet, the rumble of thunder booming.

Zerzan had slit the throat of her victim; his neck was spewing blood in an arc as she held him in front of her, using him as a shield against the men who approached from the other direction.

They were running now. I grabbed the body at my feet and hauled it in front of me.

The transport truck shook with the impact of bullets. The five men approaching from the front had learned from their friends' demise; the two women they were trying to capture were not going to go down easily.

They were running full-bore, firing at will, not aiming, just pulling the trigger. Blue scooted in behind me, both of us protected by the dead body.

I didn't have enough bullets to make many mistakes.

The first fighter to run out of rounds stopped his charge and began to reload.

He was still too far away to hit.

Zerzan was crouched down holding the jacket of the man she'd killed, keeping him in front of her. Her eyes were bright and there was a smile on her face.

The four men still running at us shot the truck as though it were their enemy.

A few more seconds and they'd be close enough for me to hit them.

I sucked in deep breaths, the stench of blood, smoke, and gasoline thick in the air. Adrenaline raced through my veins, lending me power and energy.

No pain in my ankle, no fear in my breast, no grief; I was pure action, nothing to live for, no thought of dying. There was no past and no future. Just that moment. Just each breath.

The first man stepped within my range and stopped on the road almost as if he was trying to be easier to shoot. As he took out the magazine of his rifle, I rested my right forearm on the shoulder of the dead man in front of me.

I couldn't get a clear shot with the truck in the way and so I stood up, no longer shielded by the dead body, and moved toward the front of the truck.

The fighter saw my movement and our eyes touched for a moment before I put a bullet into his brain. The other men saw me too and I ducked back behind the truck, using one of the big tires as protection.

Blue stayed flat on the ground, leaning hard into the dead body

Bullets shook the truck and I waited.

When the firing subsided slightly I peered under the truck to see one of the men had lowered his weapon to reload. Dropping onto my stomach I rolled under the vehicle and fired at him.

The bullet struck him in the thigh; blood bloomed on his pants as he fell to his knees with a scream. The pavement in front of me exploded, chunks of it flying into my face.

Ignoring the debris I aimed at the man's face. His head flipped back and he landed on the road, lying still.

Three left. Two close enough to hit. I shot one knee and the man tripped forward. As he fell, I shot the second one in the thigh.

They were both on the road grabbing at their wounds. Pop, one head flipped back. I took aim at the second man. His weapon was aimed at me. I pulled my trigger right before he did. His body fell back, his gun arced skyward releasing bullets into the air. It continued to fire, shaking his corpse, until the magazine emptied.

There was one man left and he stood in the road, surveying the carnage for only a second before turning and running back toward the burning Humvee.

Footsteps pounded on the blacktop and Zerzan came into view, sprinting after him. I stood up and raced around the truck to watch her. She was nuts, chasing down a man with a machine-gun carrying only a knife. She was also really fast. The man, weighed down by his bullet-proof vest and unwieldy rifle, was too slow.

He turned and looked back at her when she was still too far away to touch him.

He brought his gun around. The pavement to Zerzan's left exploded. Then bullets took chunks of the road right in front of her. Only a few paces from him, she leapt and flew through the air straight for his neck, knife point out.

He fired his weapon into the hillside as he opened his arms, looking as though he planned to embrace her. They fell to the ground, Zerzan on top, and thunder boomed through my mind as lightning sizzled across my vision.

EK

The knife was her father's. It had a bone handle and a pointed blade that was serrated half way down. Zerzan showed it to me, turning the weapon over in her hand, as she rinsed off the blood. The blade caught the light from the Humvee fire and lightning flickered off of it. I blinked, trying to clear it.

"How did you know he wouldn't shoot you?"

"I didn't." Zerzan's attention stayed on the weapon in her hands. "My father always told me that it was important to be brave but that it could get you killed. I am not like these men." Zerzan gestured with her knife, water spraying off the tip. "I do not think there is Heaven waiting for me. I do not believe that once I am gone, I'll meet some type of greater glory. This..." She looked up at me, seeing if I understood what "this" meant: this place, this plane of existence, this life. I nodded. "This is all it will ever be and so I don't think that God protects me, but I do think that something does. I am not afraid to die. But I do not think a man with a gun will kill me."

"What do you think will kill you?"

"I don't know, but not one of these men. Their beliefs are what keep me safe. To them, I am the Tigress. I am an otherworldly being whom they cannot kill. And so." She shrugged. "I cannot die at their hands."

The truck was destroyed. The tires blown out, the engine riddled with bullets. So we had to walk. We gathered our supplies out of the bed and started again toward the military compound. The Humvee continued to burn, but the flames did not reach as high.

"Won't someone come looking for whoever was in there?"

"Yes, maybe they will give us a ride."

As we approached the burning vehicle, I tried to see through the smoke and identify how many bodies were inside. But the interior was shrouded by the thick plumes of smoke.

We gave the burning wreckage a wide berth. Blue sneezed and shook himself.

The moon rose and the clouds parted, lighting our way. My hands were shaking slightly from the adrenaline rush. I gripped one of the rifles we'd taken off the dead men to steady myself.

Zerzan had a machine gun on her back and carried another, same as me. We'd reloaded them and taken the extra rounds that we found. I had briefly looked at the faces of the dead men; they were young, very young. One of them could barely grow a beard. It was horrifying that this is what they'd chosen.

I know some people feel the same about me. That I chose violence as a path to justice undoes any good my actions may cause. Those dead men believed in their cause the same way I believe in mine. The same way Zerzan believes in hers. Such unbending beliefs are wreaking havoc on our world, but I don't know how to reconcile it. Because I can't see any non-violent way to stop these stupid young men. Perhaps in some future, better world, men will be brought up differently and seek peaceful and diplomatic solutions to conflicts. Right now, in this moment, there was nothing to do but kill them.

"When did your father give you the knife?" I asked Zerzan as we trudged along the side of the road. My ankle was throbbing again now that the battle was over, so our pace was slow.

"He didn't give it to me. He died with it in his hand. One of his soldiers brought it to me when he came to tell us that my father was dead."

"He died in battle."

"Yes, he was a platoon leader, like me. His men were very loyal. Many of them still fight. He sacrificed himself to save them. That is what a true leader does."

"I agree. But sometimes it's important for the leader to sacrifice others."

Zerzan turned to look at me. "What do you mean?"

"A friend, at least someone I know and work with and sort of respect..." She raised her eyebrows at me in question. "It's complicated. But he gave me shit for always sacrificing myself but never willingly sacrificing others. A true leader is someone who trusts their decision making enough to know that losing people is a part of the game. It's like chess. Sometimes you have to sacrifice a pawn or even a knight to capture the king."

"Do you believe that?"

"I guess not. I'm here because I was trying to protect those around me."

"What do you mean?"

I turned my attention to the ground under my feet and bit my lip. Zerzan didn't need to know the details of how I'd arrived here or who I really was, but I wanted to tell her.

"I was blackmailed. Declan Doyle threatened to reveal my true identity." I looked up at her. "I'm Joy Humbolt."

She nodded, her face that same serene mask.

"I didn't kill Kurt Jessup."

Her eyes narrowed.

"Do you know the myth?"

"That you avenged your brother's death by killing the Mayor of New York, then escaped to start Joyful Justice."

"That's not what really happened. I didn't kill Jessup. He was already dead when I arrived at his office. I was just stupid enough to leave evidence behind that made it super easy to frame me. Robert Maxim, a very powerful and dangerous man, arranged Jessup's death. Not to avenge my brother, but for his own reasons. Mainly that Jessup was out of control and Bobby doesn't do well with people he can't control. And I didn't start Joyful Justice either. I was in a hallucinatory fog."

Zerzan's eyebrows rose in question.

"I got doused with Datura. It's a dangerous hallucinogen that is used in Colombia to rob people. It makes you totally pliable on the outside and on the inside, you see horrible, dark, scary things. I was completely out of it when Joyful Justice executed its first mission. I didn't even want it to exist. I thought it was crazy."

"And now?"

"Now I'm here. Willing to die to protect a lie. To keep Joyful Justice going."

"I think Joyful Justice is a good thing."

I laughed. "From one terrorist to another."

Zerzan nodded and smiled.

We walked in silence for another half-hour before headlights appeared in the distance.

CHAPTER NINE

It was a convoy of three Humvees. They slowed when their headlights hit us and then came to a stop. Diesel fumes wafted over us. In the open backs of the vehicles, soldiers aimed mounted machine guns at us.

Zerzan, Blue, and I stood on the sandy shoulder, waiting.

A voice came over a bullhorn. "Sydney Rye?"

"Yes," I yelled.

The passenger side door of the lead Humvee opened and a woman I didn't recognize got out, followed by Sazan, my translator.

They came around, walking through the headlights, their shadows long and distorted on the road.

The stranger was a little taller than me and broader, wearing a khaki camouflage uniform and a matching hat.

Why wasn't she in battle gear? I had assumed they were going to check on the exploded Humvee. The woman put her hand out. "Major Gabby Garcia," her accent was southern, maybe Texan. "We've been looking for you."

"Sydney Rye." I shook her hand.

"What happened?"

"Story is a little long for retelling on the side of the road. But there is a Humvee back there that hit an IED. I'm sorry, but there were no survivors."

The major frowned and looked back at her convoy. "We'll take you back to base. Just give me a second."

Sazan was chewing on her lip, watching the major's back as she headed over to speak with the driver of the second Humvee. "How are you?" I asked.

Sazan ventured a smile, her lips still tight, her eyes looking a wee bit panicked. "I'm fine. How are you?"

"Same old, same old." *Except that I'm going completely insane.*

"Have you seen Mujada?" Sazan asked, letting the smile fade from her face and taking a tentative step toward me, her voice a low whisper.

"Not for a while."

Sazan eyed Zerzan for a moment before continuing. "Do you know if she's alive?"

"As far as I know. I have not seen her for a couple days. But I didn't see her die. Just to make that totally clear."

I looked up at the stars. Did the dead watch us? Did they judge us?

Sazan chewed on her lower lip. "They say that she abducted you."

"Yup."

An asteroid entered the atmosphere, causing a vivid white streak in the sky as it burst into flame, then dissolved into nothingness.

The major called over. "Come on, you'll ride with me."

No one asked about Zerzan. Was it because they knew who she was or just didn't care? Maybe I was so important I got to bring along whomever I wanted? Or maybe it was a trap? I always did like a good trap.

EK

Declan, with his brow furrowed and eyes glittering, was waiting for me when we arrived at the base. He opened the door of the Humvee and wrapped his hand around my bicep. Blue let out a soft growl of warning and Declan looked at him, his eyes hard. Blue's lip rose, vibrating above sharp teeth.

"I'd let go."

Declan looked at his hand wrapped around my arm before releasing it. "We need to talk." He was still leaning in the Humvee and I picked up the scent of soap and the musk of sex. Declan wasn't one to let work get in the way of a carnal opportunity.

"Fine. Let's talk." Declan stepped back and I got out of the Humvee. "Can I have some water for Blue and a cup of coffee for me? Zerzan, do you want anything?" She was climbing out of the Humvee after me.

"We need to talk first, alone; then we can have a tea party." Declan fisted his hands, trying to keep from grabbing me.

"Okay, let's go."

Declan turned to Zerzan. "You can wait in the mess hall."

Sazan came up to us. "I can look after her."

Declan strode quickly across the road. I was still moving slowly because of my ankle and when Declan noticed I wasn't keeping up, he turned back, a scowl on his face. He saw my limp and cocked his head. "I sprained my ankle."

"How many people died in the bombing? And you sprained your ankle?"

"Hey, you say that like I had something to do with the bombing. I sprained my ankle before that attack, first of all. Not that it even matters. Because the two things are not connected."

Declan took a deep breath and closed his eyes for a second before turning around and continuing.

I followed him through an unlocked door and we entered a gymnasium that stank of old sweat and was littered with exercise equipment. He led me through the wide-open space to another hallway, and finally into a small room that looked a lot like an interrogation room.

It had no windows just a table with two chairs. There were metal loops in the ground that you could run shackles through. The door could be dead bolted from the outside. Blue and I stopped in the entryway and Declan turned around to look at us. "What's the matter?"

"I get claustrophobic. Is there a bigger room we can talk in?"

"You get claustrophobic? This from the woman who traveled through underground tunnels to the mayor's office to shoot him."

"Yeah. I do."

He rested his hands on the table, turning his back to me, and took several deep breaths. "This is a good place to talk; it's private. We can leave the door open."

"Okay, and I sit by the door."

"Whatever."

Blue sat by my side, his head hovering above the table as he stared across at Declan.

"So, what happened?" Declan asked.

"I was going to ask you the same thing. Because I got hit in the head and was knocked out, so I don't really understand how Mujada could have single-handedly abducted me."

"What do you mean? She hit you and you went down like a bag of bricks. I tried to grab you but Blue," Declan pointed to the dog, "seemed to think you should go with Mujada. Considering she was also holding a gun on me and keeping you in front of her body as a shield and the base was under attack, I had to let her take you."

"Then what?"

"I want you to tell me about the bombing. We lost some really good men. And Mary is gone. You don't know what that means, but it's very serious. This was her operation."

"So now it's yours?"

"Now it's over. Losing her, the only female director at Homeland Security, in what appears to be a Russian bombing of a terrorist group on land in the Iraqi-Syria conflict zone. Can you get what that means?"

"Can you just tell me?"

Declan blew air through his lips, vibrating them. "There are rules."

"They're all sorts of crazy rules. According to Daesh, there are rules that women need to cover their entire bodies and submit to sex against their will. According to the US government, there are rules that say I am a terrorist and should be in jail. There are rules that say all sorts of fucked up shit. So what rules actually count around here?

Declan's face was getting red. He looked seriously pissed off. "You are not supposed to be here. You're not even supposed to be alive."

"Were you supposed to kill me? Was Mary? Was Mujada?"

"No. Jesus. Fuck. Joy Humbolt has been dead for years. Remember?"

"Mary asked me to come here. To try and help figure out how to get women to join this fight because those Daesh idiots think that if a woman kills them, they don't get into Heaven. I came here trying to do what Mary asked. I got abducted." I raised my eyebrows, hinting that maybe, just maybe, that was a little bit his fault. Declan shook his head. "Through that abduction I met the exact people Mary needed for her idea to work."

"What 'exact people'?"

"You know, the Tigress?"

"One of the martyrs; her picture is in the mess hall. Along with yours."

"She, like me, isn't dead. The Tigress is the woman I rolled up with."

"She is a member of the FKP?"

"I can't keep any of those acronyms straight. They all seem to overlap each other anyway. She is a female fighter that is taking on Daesh in a way the US government wants. She inspires other women to fight for her. Unfortunately, most of her platoon was just killed in that Russian bombing."

"So you see the problem."

"What?"

"Mary was killed by the Russians while in the company of a platoon of terrorists."

"I prefer to see them as freedom fighters—and they hate ISIS even more than we do. But I am sorry that Mary is gone. I liked her."

"Being sorry has nothing to do it. This is an international incident."

"Can't you just lie about how Mary and her men died?" Declan's eyes narrowed. "What? Like you guys don't lie all the time?"

"What happens if the Russians find out? We'd have to explain what she was doing in FKP territory."

"Really? You'd have to explain that? I don't see why."

Declan slammed his fist on the table and Blue barked a warning. "You don't see why it's a big deal. Mary is dead. Ten of our best soldiers with her. And you're telling me that the rescue mission they went on, the one where they went to save your ass—that you didn't need saving.

In fact, you've teamed up with the woman who fucking arranged to kidnap you!"

"When was the last time you slept?"

Declan laughed. "What are you talking about now?"

"You just lost someone close to you. Obviously there's a lot of politics involved. It's stressful. And you're acting mildly insane. So I'm just wondering if maybe you haven't slept. I know I lose touch with reality when I haven't slept." *Or get hit on the head too many times.*

Declan rubbed his face and then ran his fingers through his hair. "You have to disappear. We need to get you out of here."

"Zerzan is the key to what we're talking about doing here."

"That's over. It was Mary's project. There is no interest in the program any longer. Bringing you on board was highly illegal, and I was under orders from a superior when I did it. So it's over."

"Okay, I'll just be on my way then."

"I'm not letting you go. I'm going to take you to prison. Where you belong." Declan's eyes were bloodshot and he looked wild.

"I don't think so."

"Yes, you are, and so is Zerzan. You're both terrorists." A vein in his neck pulsed. "And you are both going to be interrogated and imprisoned, and most likely you'll die there."

I smiled and shook my head. "Nah, that's not what's going to happen."

"You're in the middle of a military base, you have a sprained ankle, one gun, and you think that you're getting out of here?" He put both hands on the table and leaned forward, almost standing. "You don't even know where you are. I'm the one in charge now. I'm the one in control." He was looming over me.

"You know what your problem is, Declan?"

"I'm not the one with the problem?"

"Yeah. You are." I slipped the pistol from the waist of my pants and aimed under the table. Declan saw my arm move and reached for his own weapon but I fired before he got the chance. The force of the bullet knocked him back into his chair, his eyes closed and mouth parted releasing a sharp gasp of breath.

Then he was going for his weapon again.

"Move another millimeter and I will end you."

Declan froze, a pained grimace on his face.

"I've heard stomach wounds are the worst. But you have a chance of survival. With a head wound?" I clucked my tongue, standing up slowly. The legs of my chair scraped against the floor, sounding almost like a strong gust of wind whipping through my hair. "I was telling you about your problem. Can you guess what it is?"

"The bullet in my stomach." His normally velvety voice was rasped with pain.

I shrugged. "Fine, you have two problems. That's a new one. Your original problem was that you still think I'm Joy Humbolt." I paused for effect. "But she's dead."

Blood dripped on the floor, seconds ticking on a clock. "You try to stop me from leaving this place and I will kill you. Are we clear?"

Declan nodded. I pulled his side arm off him and laid my empty gun on the table. "You know," I caught Declan's gaze. "I wasn't even sure I had a round left when I shot you. I'd lost count. I guess the gods were on my side."

"Go to hell."

"You too."

EK

I stashed Declan's pistol before Blue and I walked out into the night, headed toward the mess hall.

I passed a group of women who were chatting under the yellow glow of an exterior light. They nodded at me and I nodded back, keeping my eyes off their weapons, feeling conscious of the fact that they might be ordered to use them on me soon.

The mess hall was mostly empty, just a few small groups of women sat around having tea and desserts. Zerzan was with Sazan and the major. She caught my eyes and I gave a slight shake of my head before turning and stepping back outside.

Zerzan came around the side of the building a few minutes later. "We need to go," I whispered.

Zerzan followed my gaze to the front gate where armed guards stood. Zerzan had just her knife and I only had Declan's handgun; we'd given up our rifles when the major picked us up. Not only were our weapons paltry compared to what we were up against, but I also didn't want to hurt any of the soldiers here. We weren't even on opposing sides. Everyone here wanted the same thing: defeating Daesh.

"Did anyone recognize you?" I asked Zerzan.

"I'm not sure."

"How did Mujada get me out?"

"We have allies here." Zerzan started walking back along the side of the mess hall, Blue and I followed.

A side door opened and the major stepped out. She saw us approaching and smiled. "What are you two doing?" She asked her hand lingering on her pistol. "Where's Declan?"

"Declan? He was exhausted. Needed a nap."

"Really?" the major said. "And what was the conclusion of your conversation?"

She went for her gun and Blue went for her arm. She didn't have a chance. The major was on the ground, Blue attached to her forearm. Her grip on the pistol lost, it tumbled across the road.

Zerzan dropped onto the major. Putting her knees on the woman's shoulders and her knife to her throat.

"Don't," I said. "Don't kill her."

"I won't. We should take her with us, for insurance."

"Great idea. Funny, I hardly ever think of abduction, but it really is a useful tool."

I called Blue off and Zerzan hauled Major Garcia to her feet. I patted her down and found a pistol in an ankle holster and a knife at her waist. She was staring at me with narrowed eyes and a deep frown. "You'll never get out of here alive."

"You have no idea how many times I've heard that."

Zerzan laughed. "Me too."

Zerzan put her knife away and pushed Garcia's pistol into the woman's stomach, keeping a tight grip on her bicep. Blue flanked the major so that she had nowhere to go.

We hurried down the road. Zerzan turned left and the motor pool appeared ahead of us: a small, squat, square structure on the edge of a large parking lot lined with vehicles.

We got to the office and Zerzan opened the door. There was a woman inside, standing at her desk holding a clipboard. She had a pencil between her teeth and long, dark hair pulled back into a neat ponytail.

She looked up as we came in and taking the pencil out of her mouth said. "Major?"

Zerzan spoke in her native tongue and the woman nodded before going to the back of the room, opening a lockbox on the wall, and pulling out a set of keys.

She handed them to me and Zerzan gestured with her chin to a side door that led out to the parking lot.

The keys were for the closest Humvee. I climbed into the driver's seat. The major, Zerzan, and Blue got in the back.

The Humvee was wider and higher than anything I'd ever driven. The big diesel engine rumbled to life when I turned the key. The powerful vibrations matched the tone of the thunder rippling at the edges of my mind.

Riding in something so high and big and strong provided the illusion of safety. But I had recently seen how an IED could send it twisting through the air with the greatest of ease.

I pulled out of the parking space, and as I drove onto the road, Zerzan directed me to the exit Mujada had taken me through. Not as large, but just as fortified as the one we'd entered.

Soldiers stood guard, their stances relaxed, the night sky sparkling above them.

"What do we do about them?"

Zerzan pressed her pistol into the major's temple, wrinkling her skin. "That is what a hostage is for."

At the gate, one of the soldiers approached us. Her rifle was up and she was yelling something.

I took my hands off the wheel and held them up. I looked down at the window control, then back up at the guard, then down at the control again, making it clear that I was going to move my hands before I did.

I rolled down the window and Zerzan spoke.

The other guard was on Zerzan's side of the car, her rifle aimed into the backseat.

The major yelled, "Shoot them."

Zerzan yelled louder. The young woman in front of me flicked her gaze between me, Zerzan, Blue, and the major before finally stepping back. The other guard did the same. They looked at each other through the vehicle. Then raised their guns to the sky. The major groaned. "Fuck."

The first guard stepped up to the control booth and opened the gate. The road stretched out before us and I gunned it. The big engine responded with an aggressive growl and we shot out into the night.

I kept checking our rearview, but no one seemed to be following us. After twenty minutes, I pulled over.

"Let's get rid of her," I said to Zerzan turning in my seat to look at the major.

Zerzan's pistol was still pressed to the woman's temple. "You don't want to kill her?" she asked.

"No. Just let her go," I answered. "I left Declan in the interrogation room by the gymnasium. Shot in the stomach. Maybe you can save his life," I said to the Major.

"You bitch."

"He was threatening me, and I had no choice."

"It was a choice."

"You're right. I chose to save myself instead of him. I chose me. Now get out of my Humvee."

"I'll find you. I will track you down."

"Why? Don't you realize we're all fighting for the same thing? We all have a common enemy. And yet you're acting like Zerzan and I are the problem."

"You're terrorists."

"So are you. You think you haven't struck terror into the hearts of the people who live here? Don't you think bombs raining down from unmanned drones is fucking terrifying? Because I can tell you, as someone who was recently bombed in a drone attack, it's real scary."

Zerzan opened her door and climbed out, dragging the major with her. The older woman stumbled and Zerzan kicked her to the ground. Blue was standing on the seat and he barked, his tail wagging. Zerzan aimed her gun at the woman's face. The major stared up at her defiantly.

"Under different circumstances, you'd probably get along with us just fine," Zerzan said.

"I'm a patriot, and that woman," she thrust her chin in my direction, "is a traitor."

Zerzan kicked the major and she arched her back away from the pain. Zerzan climbed back into the Humvee and I hit the gas, headed in the direction I was going, with no idea of what came next.

CHAPTER TEN

"Where are we going?" I asked Zerzan.

"We'll join another platoon; they are not far. A day and half, maybe two."

"Another platoon?"

"Yes, FKP has many troops in this area. My platoon was one of many."

"I think that you should come with me and we should go back to my base and figure out what you need and how to get it for you."

"Where is your base?"

"A day and a half, maybe two of travel." I smiled. My route involved plane travel, but it was the same amount of time.

"I can't leave."

"Zerzan, you're a leader. It is your job to make sure that your forces can continue fighting. You have to marshal resources and find new allies. Going headfirst into another fight does not make sense for you or your people." *Well, didn't I just sound like the most reasonable person in the stolen Humvee.*

Zerzan kept her eyes focused on the road ahead. The sky was clear and the moon was bright. Our headlights hit the road, making the sand scattered over the blacktop sparkle. "I can't leave."

"Why didn't you dispute the video Daesh made where they claimed to kill you?"

"What does that have to do with anything?"

"Just tell me."

"I enjoy being a ghost. It is safer in its way."

"So it is safer to stay, to continue the fight. I am asking you to be braver than that. I understand that you're worried about abandoning your troops. But you'd come back. And you'd bring weapons, more fighters, and intelligence with you."

"How can you promise me those things? How would we even get out of here?"

"I was hoping you could figure that out, but if not I can make some phone calls."

"The airspace is impossible to penetrate without permission. The Americans, the Russians, the Iraqis, and the Turks are all watching. Additionally, ISIS has weapons that can take aircrafts down. We could go over land, but that it is very difficult terrain and the borders are hellish. They are clogged with refugees. There's no way to leave that is easy."

"I think I know someone who can help."

"Even if you can find a way out, I'm not going."

"Don't you think that it's important? Can't you see that everything you're asking for is outside this place?"

"You don't understand." Zerzan looked over at me again and I took my eyes off the road to catch her gaze. Were her eyes teary? No, it was just a trick of the low light. "Even if we can get out, how will I get back in? It's just too risky for me."

I returned my attention to the road.

If a woman who charged a man firing a machine gun with nothing but a knife said my plan was too risky, it must be totally insane.

"Let me make a phone call," Zerzan said. "Mujada should be with the platoon I suggested we join. I will get a clearer location."

Zerzan pulled out one of the burner flip phones we'd taken off the Daesh fighters and dialed.

The voice that answered was a man's. Zerzan's mouth fell into a deep frown. She said something in her native tongue, her voice low and gravelly. The man answered her and her scowl deepened.

Zerzan responded and the man laughed. Zerzan hung up and pushed the mobile phone back into her pocket. "What happened?"

"Mujada is being held hostage. And they want to exchange her for me."

I slowed to a stop and put the Humvee into park. The engine purred, waiting for my next command.

"Where is she?"

"Not far. Maybe a day of travel." Zerzan's voice was hollow, almost echoing with emptiness.

"Only a day, that's an improvement."

"Will you come? Will you help me?" She wasn't the type to ask for help. She wanted to be the one helping. But I was her only ally here.

"Yes, I'll help. But we probably need more weapons."

"Yes, we probably do."

"I happen to know the location of a very well-stocked armory."

Zerzan's lips twitched into a smile. "And I happen to know a major who can get them for us."

I twisted the wheel, executing a tight U-turn that made Blue fall into the door, and Zerzan press against him. Zerzan said something in her native tongue that sounded like a curse.

I was driving fast, the Humvee eating up the road beneath us as we raced back in the direction we'd come.

We spotted Garcia walking along the side of the road. When she saw our headlights, she broke into a run, heading into the scrubby trees. I slammed on the brakes when we reached where she'd entered the bush, and, throwing the Humvee into park, I jumped out of it.

I released Blue with the command to take down the major. He took off into the wilderness, his white tail a streak of light as he disappeared into the brush.

I followed him at a slower pace, not wanting to injure my ankle again.

Blue barked. He'd captured her. Zerzan yelled to me when she reached them and a few moments later, I came upon the scene.

Major Garcia was on the ground with Blue standing over her. His front paws weighted down her shoulders and his face was inches from hers. Blue's lip quivered above his teeth and a low growl emanated from his breast. The major stared back at Blue, her mouth set into a straight line and her body tense beneath him.

Zerzan was next to them, her pistol pointed at the Major. I called Blue off and he bounded to my side, tail wagging. I stroked his head and told him that he was a "good boy."

The major eyed me, her expression defiant. "What now?"

"Well, we felt bad about leaving you out here. Figured it wasn't safe. So we want to give you a ride back to the compound." She stared at me, her expression unchanged. "You can get up now, let's go back to the truck."

"I'm not going anywhere with you. If you want me, you can drag me."

"Really?"

I looked over at Zerzan. The anger, driven by the fear she had for Mujada, radiated off of her. "Should I just kill her?"

The major didn't seem worried. I had to admire her. We'd abducted her, dropped her on the side of the road, then come back and chased her down, my giant dog taking her to the ground. Now Zerzan, looking like an ice cold killer, was aiming the major's own gun at her, but she was refusing to cooperate.

"Bring her along." Blue bounded back over to the major and gave a short bark. When she didn't respond he nipped at her feet. She twisted away from him but didn't get up.

Blue kept going, barking and nipping, pushing her with his nose. When she lashed out at him, Blue caught her wrist in his mouth and looked over at me. She threw her free fist and hit him in the side.

Blue dug his teeth into her tendons and yanked hard enough that she tipped over. He dragged her by her hand as she screamed.

"Release." Blue let go and returned to my side, blood staining the white fur around his mouth. The Major cradled her wrist to her chest as she sat up.

"Ready to go now?"

"I won't endanger my soldiers. I would rather die."

"Well, if she wants to die, who are we to stop her?" Zerzan asked.

"I get you," I said to the major. "How many people do you have with you?"

"I'm not telling you anything. I'm not doing anything you want me to do. And I'm certainly not helping you breach our base."

"You keep saying that as if the base is American. It's Iraqi."

"Kurdish." Zerzan corrected me.

"Iraqi." The major corrected Zerzan.

Zerzan's finger tightened on the trigger.

"Well, in any case, it's not American. We can all agree on that."

"Those women are my allies and I'm not going to let you hurt them."

"For the record, I was your ally not so long ago. Did you know Mary Leventhal?" The major didn't answer. "Do you know what she was doing here? What I was doing here?"

"I know who you are, and I know where you belong."

"Who do you think I am?"

"A member of Joyful Justice. You're a terrorist. And you should be locked up."

"The thing is, Mary brought me here. Obviously, I didn't come here of my own free will. Why would I?"

"You're working with FKP. Another terrorist organization," she sneered, looking over at Zerzan.

"I get you think we're bad news," I said.

"Bad news? I don't think you're *bad news,* I think you're dangerous criminals."

"Worse than Daesh? Come on, do you think we're on their side? Can't we agree that the enemy of my enemy is my friend?"

The major laughed. "If you were my friends, you wouldn't have needed to escape from a military base. You wouldn't have shot Declan Doyle. I wouldn't be bleeding." She held up her torn wrist.

"We're actually very much alike."

The major laughed again. Her shirt was soaking with blood. "We are nothing alike. I have spent my life working my way up the ranks of the U.S. Army. My life has been about discipline and following orders and working for the good of my nation. You are terrorists. You're not going to convince me to help you."

I looked over at Zerzan. She was staring down the barrel of her pistol at the woman. "I say drag her."

"Go ahead," the major dared us.

"What was Mary's reputation?"

"What?" The major asked, confused by my quick change in topic. Blue tapped my hand with his nose, waiting for his next command, sensing that it was coming soon.

"What was Mary's reputation?"

"She was a tough, smart, out-of-the-box thinker."

"Would you trust her with your life? Would you trust her with your soldiers' lives?"

"Yes, we were on the same side."

"She trusted me."

"And look how that turned out."

"I, unlike you, don't have access to drones or bombs. I tried to save her." I could still smell the stench of that fire: caustic plastic, roasting flesh, and coppery blood.

"I don't know what happened. I wasn't there."

I shook my head, looking down at the woman. Her soft jowls, hard eyes, thin, brown hair in disarray—she'd lost her hat somewhere along the way. This was the problem with the world. So stuck in her beliefs, just like me, so stuck in mine. The big difference: I was right.

"Okay, Blue." His body vibrated with excitement. His tail swinging back and forth as he awaited my next words. "Bring her along."

The major began to rise, getting up to her knees.

Blue barked and circled her nudging her back with his nose and nipping at her heels. She stood slowly, blood from her wrist dripping off her elbow. Blue continued to bark at her and she lashed out, trying to kick him. Blue dodged and launched himself onto her back, knocking her face first into the dirt. She landed with a thud. Blue grabbed the collar of her shirt and began to yank her down the hill. Her face was in the dirt, dragging through the land.

"Ready to walk?" I asked. She couldn't respond. "Blue, hold on." Blue stopped but kept his teeth locked onto her collar.

"Get up."

The major rose to her hands and knees. Her breathing was short and dirt fell off her face and hair. I grabbed her arm and hauled her up. She didn't try to get loose. "We're gonna get you to the truck. You might as well walk."

"No."

Zerzan grabbed her other arm and we dragged her back down the hill to the waiting Humvee. She didn't so much walk as stumble between us.

The Humvee stood as we'd left it, with the front doors open, engine rumbling, headlights sending white columns through the night. Lightning fissured around it and thunder made the road tremble under my feet.

EK

I found a first aid kit in the back of the Humvee and wrapped up the major's wrist.

Blue was excited by the turn of events. His tail was wagging against the seat as he watched me tend to the wounds. There were puncture marks that had torn up her wrist, leaving wide gashes. Blood came out as quickly as I blotted it away. I packed sterile gauze against the cuts and then wrapped more around it. "You're going to need stitches." She didn't respond. "I get why you don't want to help us but I'd like to tell you why we came back and then you can decide if you want to keep up not helping."

"There is nothing you can say that will change my mind."

"I kind of feel that's one of the big problems we have in the world right now. If we all refuse to listen, how will anything ever change?" The major turned her gaze to look out the window. "Well, I'll tell you anyway. A friend of ours, a brave, young woman who has spent her entire adult life fighting Daesh has been captured. And we are going to get her back."

"She doesn't care," Zerzan said.

"I care about the women that Daesh takes," the major said, her voice low, almost like she was admitting a secret. "It is horrific what is happening here."

"So you can see how it can turn a woman into a terrorist," Zerzan said, her voice dripping with condescension.

The major shook her head and cast her gaze back to the passing landscape.

"This woman, who we're going to save, she is a lot like you. Follows orders, fights for what she believes in, is willing to die to protect those around her. To protect those that she fights with."

"I'm sorry about your friend. But that doesn't change anything."

"What we need are weapons. We don't want to hurt anyone at the base. I shot Declan because of something between us. We didn't hurt anyone else on our way out."

"Only because you didn't have to." The major raised her bandaged wrist. "You're not afraid to hurt people to get what you want. I'm not risking my soldiers around you."

"Aren't you the same?"

She smiled. "No. I'm not the same. Going into extreme danger to save one person. That's not a strong mission. That cannot win this war."

"You think you know what will win this war?" Zerzan asked, her voice an angry growl. "You are an idiot. So many of you Americans think you know how to solve our problems. And all you do is make it worse. All you've ever done is make it worse."

The major was about to respond when I laid a hand on her arm and shook my head. "Listen to me, I want to be real clear about what I'm asking for. You don't have to put anyone in danger. You just have to supply us with weapons."

"Supplying you with weapons is dangerous. How do I know they won't be used against me or any of my troops?"

"You have my word."

"You're supposed to be going to a holding facility."

"What if I promise to come back?"

Zerzan stiffened in the driver's seat.

"I don't believe you."

"I promised Declan I would let him lock me up. That's how we got here in the first place."

"Right. Then you shot him to prevent that from happening."

"That's true," I laughed, because she had a very valid point. "But we'd made a new deal at that point and I'd followed through, coming here. As you might imagine, this isn't exactly my idea of a mountain vacation. I came here at his and Mary's request to help them figure out how to get more women to fight. They wanted to create a similar pull through social media and the Internet for women as Isis has done for young men."

The major's eyes widened. "That was her plan?"

"Yes, but when she died, so did the plan. Then Declan tried to lock me up. But, at that point, I had already given my word to Zerzan that I would help her."

"That's an interesting story." The major maintained eye contact. The woman's eyes were emerald green with slashes of yellow in them. Wrinkles fanned out from them, proof of a life spent in the sun and wind. This was a woman of action. She didn't strategize behind a desk, she spent her time in the field.

The major's lip curled into a smile or a snarl; I wasn't sure until she spoke. "I love that these men believe if a woman kills them they go to Hell."

"Me too," Zerzan said.

We were fifteen minutes from the base now. "You can help us and make sure that no one gets hurt. If you don't, we will have to do it the hard way, and then I can't guarantee that bad things won't happen."

"Are you threatening me?"

"I've been threatening you basically since the moment we met."

"Not from the very beginning. Remember, I gave you a ride."

I laughed. "Right, but pretty soon after."

"I can't help you. It would be risking too much."

"The only thing you would be risking is your career."

"I fought hard to get where I am."

"And that means more to you than what's right?" I shook my head and turned away from her.

When the base came into view, I sat forward and spoke to Zerzan. "We know we can trust the women at the south gate. Let's see if they will just give us their weapons."

"They won't do that. They'd be court-martialed," Garcia said.

"Even better," I said. "Let's ask them to come with us."

EK

Zerzan came to a stop as the guards approached our vehicle. They were in the standard formation, rifles raised, circling the car. The machine guns mounted on the wall were aimed down at us. *Please let us live long enough to save Mujada.*

Zerzan rolled down her window. The guard approaching had on full fighting gear: flak jacket and helmet, handgun holstered at her hip.

The woman asked something in Kurdish and Zerzan responded.

I sat forward. "Do you recognize her?" The woman pulled the flashlight off her belt and illuminated Zerzan's face. Zerzan flinched away for a second but then looked back at the woman, staring into the light. She lifted her chin, exposing the scars on her throat. The flashlight clicked off.

"The Tigress."

"We need your help," I said.

"Anything."

"Weapons and you."

The woman's brows raised. "Me?"

"Yes, you," Zerzan said, finding her voice. "I need you and her." Zerzan pointed at the other woman holding a rifle on us. "And them." She pointed at the two dark figures manning the machine guns on the wall. "Anyone else you can trust to come with me."

"Why?"

"To kill Daesh."

"You can't just abandon your post." The major sat forward, yelling out the window. "You will leave everyone in danger."

"Our shift changes in ten minutes," the guard answered.

"We need weapons and grenades, anything we can get," I said.

"I'll let you get what you need from the armory, and then I will go with you," the guard said.

The guard on the other side of the car spoke. "I will come with you too."

"Thank you." Zerzan said, her voice strong and clear, like a church bell ringing through a town filled with the faithful.

The gate opened and we rolled through. The major sat back into the seat and shook her head. "God dammit."

"At least you didn't have to walk back here. And unless you do something spectacularly stupid in the next ten minutes, you're gonna be just fine."

"Those women are now deserters. They will face consequences."

"They may not live to face them," Zerzan stated.

We parked in front of the armory. I dragged the major out of the car with us and Zerzan held her tight, a pistol pressed into the woman's stomach as I unlocked the armory with the major's keys.

I left Blue guarding the major near the entrance as Zerzan and I ran around gathering arms. We grabbed a crate full of machine guns, hundreds of rounds, and a box of grenades. I discovered the knives and was loading a bunch into a bag when I popped open a crate and found a stash of throwing stars. They glinted in the overhead lights and I smiled, thinking of my trainer, Merl. I picked up one of the blades and weighted it in my palm. Perfect.

We loaded our booty into the Humvee.

"What should we do with her?" Zerzan asked about the major.

"Tie her up and leave her. Stick a sock in her mouth."

I bent down to get her shoe off but she kicked out at me. Blue leapt, taking her to the floor; the major's head smacked hard into the cement. She was dazed as I untied her shoe and pulled off the sock.

I flipped her over and grabbed her wrists, tying them together. She muttered something, but was incoherent as I pulled her ankles up to her wrists and joined the two.

I shoved the sock into the major's mouth.

"I want you to know that I get you. I understand why you won't help us, and there's even a small part of me that admires you. But I've learned over the years that flexibility is important when it comes to seeking justice. If your only goal in life is to move up the ranks and to become a general someday, that's great on one level.

"But if you want to actually make a difference in this world, if you want to make a difference in this fight that is happening right here for this land, then you have to recognize that continuing to blindly follow the orders handed down to you is never going to help."

The major's eyes were open and she was watching me, but her pupils appeared dilated. It wasn't clear she was following me. And even if she could, it was unlikely she'd believe me.

I stood up and Zerzan, Blue, and I returned to the Humvee.

"I know a place we can pick up food and water," Zerzan said.

"Is it a day and a half away?"

"No," Zerzan laughed. "It's much closer than that."

We returned to the gate. There were now eight guards. Shift change was happening.

Zerzan stopped the Humvee in front of the closed gate.

Three of the guards approached, including the two who had agreed to come with us. "We will come—and my friend too. The others will stay to guard the gate."

The three defecting guards climbed into the back of the Humvee and the gate opened. Zerzan pulled through and when the road split, she took a left, heading back toward the wreckage of the other Humvee and the dead bodies of the Daesh members we'd left behind.

CHAPTER ELEVEN

I introduced myself to the three women in the back. "I'm Sydney Rye," I said, smiling, trying to look friendly.

They were young and pretty, with black hair and brown eyes, thick lashes, skin the caramel color of beach sand.

The first guard to agree to help us touched her chest. "Dilsoz." She cradled her rifle in her arms and her helmet tilted over her brow, looking too big for her, almost like she was a child playing dress up.

"Erzo," said the woman sitting in the middle seat. She was taller than Dilsoz, but looked just as young. Just as vulnerable. These women were not hard like Zerzan and me. Their idealism sprung from optimism; ours grew from a darker place.

When I turned my attention to the third woman, a blush stole over her cheeks. She was shorter and curvier than the other two. I didn't recognize her, so assumed she had manned one of the guns on the wall. When I raised my eyebrows at her she spoke: "Hedar."

"Nice to meet you all."

Hedar glanced down at Blue and smiled.

"This is Blue," I said, stroking his head. Erzo touched her eye. "Yes, that's right. I named him after his eye color. Not very creative."

Erzo smiled and translated for the other two. One of them spoke and her face became serious. "It is an honor to work with the Tigress," she said, her words coming slowly, carefully, as though she'd spent time choosing each one.

"For me too," I said.

Zerzan spoke in her native tongue and the women nodded, pleased. "I told them that I understand they have risked their lives and careers to join us. And that it means a lot to me," Zerzan said, her gaze remaining on the road.

We turned off onto a dirt track. I held onto the door handle to steady myself as we bumped along. Blue's body shifted back and forth, knocking into my legs.

We reached a small village, a few houses lining the road. Zerzan stopped at the first abode, parking next to a beat-up Toyota pickup truck. "Wait here" Zerzan ordered, climbing out of the Humvee and knocking on the door of the house.

It opened and electric light spilled onto the doorstep, bathing Zerzan in its yellow glow. She stepped inside and the door closed, dropping the entrance back into shadow.

A few moments later, Zerzan returned with an older man. He had a limp; a wooden peg supported his left leg. His gait was awkward, but he moved as quickly as Zerzan.

His eyes narrowed, trying to see into the dark cab of the Humvee. He nodded at something Zerzan said and then gestured for us to get out.

Zerzan handed him the keys.

We climbed out, Blue ran over to a tree and did his business. The man climbed into the driver's seat. "Dadyar will take the vehicle and get rid of it," Zerzan said. "We will take his truck." Erzo, Dilsoz, and Hedar transferred our supplies to the rusted hulk. The taillights were broken and one of the back windows was cardboard. Beggars can't be choosers.

The three women went inside while Zerzan and I waited for Blue. The man backed the Humvee up and headed further down the road.

"What is this place?" I asked as the Humvee disappeared around a bend. I could still hear its big engine and just make out the red glow of its tail lights through the trees.

"It is a shelter for abused women. This is one of the stops on the way out of Iraq."

"Where are they going?"

Zerzan shrugged. "Once they cross the Turkish border, I do not know. It is safer for them if less people know. The women who come here, they are in grave danger. Often they must leave their children behind. Can you imagine? To flee from your husband, and yet leave a piece of your heart behind." Zerzan shook her head.

"I can't."

"I think they are very brave to run."

"Yes, it is brave to escape. But what is their other option? To stay and die?"

"Some of them would be killed by their husbands, yes. The others would just be tortured for the rest of their lives. Many women who face rape and abuse do not leave. They stay for their children. They stay because there is no guarantee of a better life. If they are caught, they will die horribly."

Blue returned to my side and we started for the front door.

"Can they fight?"

"Fight? The women who take shelter here? No. They are on the run. Afraid."

"I've found that running and leading are very closely related."

Inside Dilsoz, Hedar, and Erzo sat on one couch facing three women covered in black burkas. Every part of them was hidden, even their eyes. The fabric looked heavy, the mesh they watched me through allowed glints of light to hit their irises, making me feel like I was being watched by caged animals.

Zerzan made introductions in Kurdish and then in English. Nazdar, Rojda, and Tajev. Which was which I didn't know.

Did the burkas make them feel safe? They must be horribly traumatized by their experiences. I wanted to tear those hoods off their heads. Take them by their shoulders, stand them up, look into their eyes, and tell them to fight.

They had traveled far to come there, and yet their journey had barely begun. Why should they continue? They should stay here and be trained to fight back against what had driven them away from their own children.

My mind clicked the idea over and over, thunder crackling. It felt imperative to me that this was the answer. These women, who weren't allowed to show any part of themselves to strangers, deserved so much more. But there was no way for me or anyone else to change their lives. Or the lives of their daughters. They had to join the fight.

Zerzan was speaking to me and I apologized, asking her to repeat herself. "We will eat now and then get food and water for the journey."

The three covered women went into the kitchen and came back with plates of food for us. They brought a hunk of raw meat for Blue and a bowl of water.

The shortest of the women, her long, black robes stained at the sleeves and splattered on the skirt, giggled when Blue licked her hand as she placed the bowl of water down on the ground for him.

How old was she?

It was possible that these were not women at all, that they were only girls.

I forced food down, knowing I needed the sustenance.

"Mujada is being held about six hours from here," Zerzan explained over tea after our meal. We sat in the kitchen, at a worn, wooden table, a florescent tube flickering and humming on the wall, casting corpse-white light over the room.

"The man on the phone said that if I showed up and traded myself for her, that they would let her go. Of course, I don't believe them. They want to hold us both."

"So why would we think that Mujada is where they say she is?"

"They will show her to me. They know I would not hand myself over without proof of her being alive."

"Fair enough. So what's the plan? We go to this place, you say, 'I am here to turn myself in,' they show us Mujada, and then what?"

"It is a former US military installation. I trained there, so I know the layout. It will most likely be a surprise to them that we know the layout so well."

Blue, who'd been sleeping under the table, stood up and released a low growl. A moment later I heard the rumble of an engine. Zerzan, Blue, and I hurried into the living room. Dilsoz, Hedar, and Erzo were standing by the window, their rifles raised.

The three women in burkas linked hands and huddled together. I pulled out a handgun holding it butt out toward the closest one. "Take it."

She didn't move but the person next to her reached out. The girl's skin was revealed as her sleeve rose; a ridged scar ran from the base of her palm up her arm, and under the garment. She grabbed the gun.

"That's a safety," I pointed to the latch that armed the pistol. She clicked it off, either having done it before or having seen it done. "Just don't shoot me."

Zerzan was over by the window peering through the curtains. "It's okay," she said. "It's just Dadyar returning."

The tension released as we all exhaled. The girl offered me back the gun. She'd put the safety back into place.

"You keep it. If we had more time, I'd teach you to use it."

The woman's robed head swiveled to Zerzan who translated. The woman shook her head. "She says it is too expensive a gift."

"Tell her that one day I may ask her to do something for me. She should consider it a down payment."

Zerzan translated and the woman nodded, bowing slightly to me as she hid the weapon in her robes. Yes, this was the answer. This girl with that gun. It was the solution we needed.

CHAPTER TWELVE

Daylight filtered into the sky as we left— Blue, Erzo, Dilsoz, and Hedar in the bed of the pickup, Zerzan driving, me in the passenger seat, staring out the window, thinking about those women shrouded in cloth.

Sunlight warmed the air and gilded the trees. The three women in the back of the pickup, in their fatigues, with their rifles and steely gazes, would have intimidated anyone we passed. But we didn't pass anyone.

The map Zerzan had drawn lay on my thigh. I studied the layout of the buildings in the compound where Mujada was being held.

We would approach from the east on a road that Zerzan said was unpaved.

We'd hide the truck and go on foot, traversing through the woods. We had walkie-talkies to communicate. They were a reminder of what these fighters needed. Walkie-talkies that squawked were a dangerous tool. But they were the only ones we had.

The plan was to use them only to announce that we were in position. They made a subtle beep that could be turned off if necessary. You would have no way of knowing someone was trying to contact you, but if you were hiding, it was imperative to be able to maintain silence.

The five of us would travel together until about five km from the base, at which point Dilsoz and Hedar would go north and Erzo and Zerzan south while Blue and I continued straight west.

The two Kurdish teams would circle around and observe the compound from the north and south. The main entrance lay on the far side of the compound, to the west.

We would try to discover where Mujada was being held from a safe distance, but if that was not possible, then we would take up position, a team in each direction, while Zerzan walked into the camp to trade herself for Mujada.

Once Mujada was revealed, we would attack.

Because the compound was so isolated, it did not have cement walls, just fencing with barbwire at the top. We had bolt cutters. All of us carried knives and the plan was to stay quiet for as long as possible. If we could sneak in, grab Mujada, and sneak out, that would be ideal...sort of.

A part of me, a large part, wanted to destroy them all. To kill every asshole living at that compound. And to make sure they knew it was me before they died. To make sure that their final emotion was dread at their journey to Hell. I'd almost be willing to believe in such a place if I could send some of these dickholes to it.

Besides the not-killing-them-all part, the plan was right up my alley. I was used to more support and better equipment, as well as Dan in my ear, but I felt excited at the impending attack.

The three women I'd met at the shelter stayed at the forefront of my mind; their shrouded bodies a reminder of the freedoms that I enjoyed even as a fugitive.

My face and name were hunted but at least I knew myself and wasn't afraid of my own family. The memory of my loving and kind brother gave me strength, even if his death caused me incredible pain. While my mother and I no longer spoke and disagreed strongly on reality, she'd never tried to physically hurt me.

However, it was easy to imagine the circumstances those women had fled from because I'd known so many women who'd escaped abusive situations. But all of them had found their way to Joyful Justice, and therefore had gone from being victims to fighters.

My friend, Tanya, who'd left Moldova looking for a better life in America, was forced to become a sex slave. When given the opportunity to escape, she'd taken it. Tanya was now one of our fiercest fighters.

Unlike the women I'd met in that house, Tanya was never forced to cover herself: She was forced to expose her skin, to allow men to touch her. And in exchange, she wasn't killed—only beaten.

Those burkas, the coverings meant to keep those women safe, had not kept men at bay. Worse than strangers, their own family, the men responsible for their safety, their everything, had used them like they were blowup dolls, not even offering the same respect they'd offer livestock.

Keeping them faceless and formless made them easier to dehumanize and abuse.

While intellectually I could understand that systematic abuse broke down a person's psyche and kept them imprisoned, my gut couldn't understand how women let this keep happening. There were more of us than them! Fifty-one percent of the population is female and yet even in the most equal societies, women are not equal.

The world is designed for men even in the simplest ways, like in the public bathroom where there is no place to put a child. The world is designed for women to be at home, covered in cloth, taking care of their babies, accepting any abuse that is forced upon them. Even in western society, we have not changed that basic design.

As we rumbled through the forest in that old Toyota pickup truck, rage that started as a simmer was growing into a boil. The injustice in the world had always pissed me off, but as my mind deteriorated, it became harder to control. The starkness of those women covered from head to toe made it crystal clear to me that nowhere were women truly free.

Looking at Zerzan, her gaze on the road as she navigated over the rough path, I marveled at her strength and determination. She grew up in a society where men and women were at least attempting to be equal. She was fighting to keep that alive for herself and future generations. Mary had brought me here to figure out how to bring more women into this cause. To help create more women like Zerzan: hard, tough, and brave killers. As I thought about that fifty-one percent of the planet that remains subservient to the smaller half, I felt a note of hopelessness at the edge of my rage.

How could we change this? How would it be possible to wake women up to their power?

Joyful Justice used social media, including YouTube videos, to great effect. We were like ISIS in that respect. Almost every mission we ran was recorded, with the people who carried out the mission providing YouTube testimonials. The same people who had brought the problem to Joyful Justice's attention.

Tanya had created the first video that went viral. After she worked with Joyful Justice to free herself and the other women being held captive with her in Miami, she burned down the clubs they'd been forced to work in. In her video, Tanya stood a short distance from a low-slung building engulfed in flames. She wore a strapless, sequined dress, her thick mascara smudged around her eyes, looking like war paint. She stared into the camera, her blue-green eyes vibrant, her voice steady and strong, as she warned other evil-doers what would happen to them.

Last I'd heard, that video had over seventy million views. Tanya was on Interpol's and America's most wanted lists because of that video. All she did was kill one scumbag and destroy a shit ton of property. It was the video, encouraging others to stand up, that had been so frightening to authorities. Inciting violence. Inciting revolution.

Over the course of history, there have been successful revolutions with little bloodshed. Was it possible that women rising up to stand side-by-side with men could be one of them? I doubted it.

Zerzan navigated off the road and into the trees. The women and Blue jumped out of the bed of the truck. Zerzan and I joined them. We all shouldered our large packs, bulging with food, water, and weapons.

My ankle felt steady as we began our hike, single file, Zerzan leading, Blue and I bringing up the rear.

The weight of the pack held my shoulders in place as I leaned forward, trudging up the steep incline. Blue occasionally tapped his nose against my waist as a reminder that he was there.

The day was getting warmer and sweat pooled on my back. Zerzan stopped and turned to the group. She smiled back at us as she pulled out a bottle of water. The rest of us followed suit, drinking deeply. "Not much further now."

"How many men do you think are there?" I asked.

Zerzan shrugged. "I don't know, Sydney, the same way I didn't know the first time you asked."

"It can hold about one hundred, right?"

"Yes, but I do not think that they have so many fighters here. It is very remote. They would be foolish to keep too many men there."

I scanned over Hedar, Dilsoz, and Erzo; they looked hot under all their gear. I didn't envy their bulletproof vests on a hike.

Like Zerzan, I didn't worry about getting killed. It wasn't something that came into my mind. I worried about Blue. And I worried about these three young women in front of me. Did they have families? Mothers like Zerzan's, who thought about them every night and day, hoping they were still alive, dreading any news that might end their worlds.

We started forward again, Zerzan checking her compass as we moved through the thick foliage. It was still mostly pine trees here; however, there was more ground cover, which made the hike more difficult.

Zerzan stopped and turned back to the group. "This is where we should have some food and drink and then we will split up." We sat on the ground and pulled out the food that the women in burkas had packed for us.

We still had about another hour and half of hiking before we reached the camp. There were roads that led to it, but we didn't want to be so obvious.

Zerzan checked her cell phone. No call. Dan and I had spoken briefly, just long enough for me to tell him the plan, for him to sound nervous about it, and for me to promise to call him when it was over.

He was working on how to get me out of the country in the meantime. Though he sounded unsure if it would be necessary. For some reason, he thought me and four other fighters taking on an unknown number of soldiers in their own encampment sounded like a suicide mission.

But then again, Dan liked things to be well planned and expertly executed. Whereas flying by the seat of my pants was how I got this far in the first place. I laughed out loud at that thought and the other women looked at me. I shook my head and put up a hand. "Nothing, just a funny thought." That being here, in these woods, about to do something suicidal, was a good thing—that was funny.

The meal complete and our bags repacked, Zerzan pulled out her hand-drawn map again and we went over the plan for the final time. We checked our walkie-talkies to make sure that the communication lines were clear.

Once we were all in position, we would report in.

I had the least distance to travel, and according to Zerzan, I would be able to view the barracks from my position. I'd report what I could see. Then cut the fence and wait for the others to get into position.

I was checking my compass, looking down at the little needle as it swiveled back-and-forth, when Zerzan embraced me. I inhaled her scent: pine sap, soil, and something all her own, a smell that lingered around her, belonged to her alone.

Zerzan let me go and then turned away so that I didn't see her facial expression. "Good luck," she said.

"Be brave," I responded. It was the saying of Joyful Justice. How members greeted each other and said goodbye. Kind of our Aloha. It was a reminder that fear was expected, but bravery was cultivated.

I took a moment to look at each of the other women's faces, noting the expressions of determination they all wore, and felt secure.

Erzo and Dilsoz went in one direction, Zerzan and Hedar the other, while Blue and I continued straight. Since the other women had further to go, there was no reason for us to hurry. We stopped an hour later and had some more water. I sat on a fallen tree and closed my eyes, feeling the sun on my face and listening to the sounds of the forest: birds chirping, small creatures rustling, wind whistling.

About thirty minutes later, the fence came into view: a sparkle of metal in a sea of nature. Blue and I slowed and my body began to tingle. We moved quietly and steadily toward the fence. Once it was fully in view, we crouched down behind a fallen log.

The fence had not been maintained properly. The barbed wire was unspooled and disconnected in places. It drooped off the top of the fence like a lazy slinky. From our vantage point, we could see three different buildings, all one story. They had flat roofs and dirty windows. After ten minutes of observation, we still hadn't seen a single person. Was it because they were all out of their rooms? Or because there just weren't that many people there?

"I'm in position," I whispered into my walkie-talkie. "The fence is damaged in places. There is no sign of movement." Blue growled and I looked up to see a man outside the fence about thirty feet away. He was staring at me.

EK

The guard held a machine gun. He wore pale green pants, a matching shirt, and a hat on his head in the same color. A black and white checked scarf wound around his neck.

His dark eyes sparkled as he watched me.

Crouching on the ground, my weapon holstered, I was vulnerable. While I thought I could get out my gun and fire before he shot me, I knew the noise would alert any other combatants to my existence. I spoke into the walkie-talkie. "There are patrols in the woods."

He yelled something and I dropped the walkie-talkie, slipping a throwing star between my pointer and index fingers before showing him my empty palms.

He aimed the rifle at Blue and I quickly stepped in front of him and shook my head. He began to approach me, keeping his weapon leveled at my chest.

When he was about fifteen feet away I twisted my body, pulling my arm back and then using the torque of my return, slung the blade. It sank deep into his throat.

His eyes went wide, the whites visible all around his brown irises. He choked and fell to his knees, coughed and blood dripped from his lips. He reached up a hand and touched the blade before his eyes rolled into the back of his head and he fell forward, landing on his face in the dirt.

I picked up my walkie-talkie, then Blue and I approached him. My pistol drawn, I used my foot to flip him over. He was dead. One down.

I searched the body and found another walkie-talkie; clearly he was meant to check in at some point. I turned up the volume, hearing only static. Unsure how long we had before his absence was noted, I reported the incident to Zerzan and the others over my walkie-talkie.

I backtracked to where he'd been standing when I first spotted him. There was a path in the woods. It was just a footpath, a wearing down of the soil and pushing aside of the vegetation, but it was a route that they apparently patrolled.

I climbed down to the fence, leaving Blue on the ridge above me, and snapped the metal with my bolt cutters. Then I returned to my spot by the log and watched the compound, waiting for Zerzan and the others to reach their positions.

Zerzan's voice came over the device. "We are at the south entrance. There are three guards. A supply truck just entered. Hedar will wait here while I continue to the west entrance."

Erzo and Dilsoz also checked in. They were in position to the north. "We can see the mess hall; there are five men sitting outside smoking." Dilsoz would remain there while Erzo went around to meet with Zerzan.

"Watch for the footpaths; there are guards in the woods," I warned again.

Blue and I stared at the empty barracks and waited for Zerzan to check in again.

"Erzo and I are here. This gate is guarded by four men. They look relaxed but are well armed. I'm going to call the others now." Zerzan left the line open. She spoke in Kurdish so I couldn't understand what was being said. "They are ready for me. I will leave my walkie-talkie here. Erzo will be able to see me."

My heart beat faster and I pulled three grenades from my bag, laying them on the log next to me. I dried my hands on my pants and waited. The silence that followed was excruciating.

But then I heard yelling in the distance. Zerzan must have revealed herself to the men at the gates. There was a crack along the line and Erzo spoke. "Zerzan is at the gate. She is demanding to see Mujada. They are yelling for her to get on the ground."

I heard shots. "They are firing at her." I pulled the pin from one of the grenades and launched it into the compound. I ducked behind the log and heard the explosion and felt the heat of the blast.

More gunfire sounded. Picking up my grenades, I put them in a pocket at my waist, silenced my walkie-talkie, then ran down to the gap I'd created in the fence. Blue was by my side and as we entered the compound, his nose tapped my waist. Staying low to avoid most of the smoke pluming out of the building I'd exploded, we ran along the fence, heading north.

CHAPTER THIRTEEN

The grenade had blasted a hole in the side of the building and smoke poured from the interior. There were no signs of people running or evacuating. Blue stayed close.

The sound of gunshots had stopped, and I heard an engine approaching. I ran up to the building in front of me, across from the fence, and hunkered down with my back against the wall.

A truck pulled up to the burning building and men jumped out. A fire hose appeared in their arms and they began to extinguish the flames.

There were five of them, two on the hose while the other three began to search the area, yelling back and forth.

Blue tapped his nose to my hip. He was sniffing the air and looking west, in the direction of the gate Zerzan had entered. I nodded my head and we began to move away from the fire.

Blue and I moved slowly and cautiously, keeping our senses on high alert. Blue's ears swiveled back and forth, searching for sounds of danger. He stopped at the edge of a building and peered around. I stayed behind him.

Blue jogged across the exposed street to the next building and I followed. The street was empty. I could hear the hose and the crackle of the fire, but it was growing dimmer as we moved further into the compound.

We reached another intersection and Blue paused, his nostrils flaring. His hackles rose and I heard footsteps around the corner. I tapped my hip quietly and Blue moved behind me. Pressing my back against the wall, I stood at the very edge of the building, listening. Muffled voices. Perhaps they were inside the building and a window or door was open. I looked back at Blue; he flared his nostrils and then wagged his tail. I nodded at him, and he licked his lips as his tail picked up a faster beat.

He was excited for the battle ahead.

I stood still for about another thirty seconds, just listening. It was men's voices only. But it was possible that this was either where they had brought Zerzan or where they were holding Mujada.

Glancing down the length of the building, I saw that the windows were all closed, the curtains pulled. They were unbarred. Not much of a prison.

I peeked around the corner of the building and saw that the street was empty, the door to the building propped open. There was a window between me and the open doorway.

In the other direction was one more building and then the border fence. The building across from me appeared to be unoccupied. I crouched down and then slipped around the corner, headed for the open door, staying low so that I couldn't be seen by anyone peering out the window.

Blue was right behind me; his nose tapped my heel as I crept toward the open door. I stopped shy of the opening and took a deep calming breath.

I heard a low moan. It was sexless. Blue's tail whipped through the air.

I took another deep breath and then slowly stood, sliding my back up the exterior wall of the building. Blue's hackles puffed and his feet did a little dance as he prepared to engage.

I tapped the back of my left leg, instructing Blue to stay behind me.

He glared at me but I knew that he would obey. One more breath and then I pivoted, stepping into the open doorway my rifle up at my shoulder, eyes trained down the barrel. There were three men; they were standing around a metal cage constructed for a large dog. When they saw me one of them yelped and all three began to fumble for the guns at their waists. I shot the man closest to me. As I shifted my aim left to the next man, Blue leapt from behind me, and as I pulled the trigger, I heard his body slam into the last man.

I swung around and lowered my aim finding Blue shaking the man's arm. His weapon, a small machine gun, was still in his grip. As my gaze fell on them, the man pulled the trigger. Bullets blasted into the cement floor at my feet, sending up chunks of debris and dust.

I dove to the left, landing next to one of the dead men. On my belly, I brought my rifle back to my shoulder, aimed at the man's head, and fired.

His body went limp; the weapon slipped out of his hand and Blue backed away, his mouth red with the dead man's blood.

I closed the door and pushed the deadlock into place then turned my attention to the dog cage; inside was a naked figure. The back was to me; it was covered in seeping wounds. Long lashes, some welts, others lines of torn skin crusted with dried blood.

The body was in the fetal position so that the head was down between the shoulders, but I could see knotted, black hair. It was Mujada.

Blue was by the cage, his nose pressed between the bars and he was whining.

Revulsion and white-hot anger broiled inside of me. I approached the cage and found the door padlocked. I crouched down near Mujada's head. "Hey, it's Sydney."

There was no response. Her breathing was shallow and her face was covered in her hair. Cigarette burns dotted her arms. Black, brown, purple, green, and blue bruises mottled her legs. They looked like storm clouds.

I needed to find the keys to the padlock.

I searched the closest body. It was the man Blue had taken down. His head wound was leaking onto the floor, and I stepped into the puddle to get to his pockets. He wore loose navy pants that cinched at the ankle and a button down shirt. In his pocket I found a cell phone and some hard candies but no key. I pocketed the cell phone and moved on to the next man. I'd shot him in the chest, and he lay on the ground with his arms flung wide. His eyes were open and staring at the ceiling. He was young.

There was soft stubble on his jaw and a dusting over his lip. He could not have been much over eighteen.

I looked back at Mujada's body and the wounds that covered her which made it easier to fight back a stab of guilt. It wasn't my fault this boy had chosen to be here, but it was my fault he was dead.

He didn't have the keys either.

The third body was a slightly older man but still young. He had a large Adam's apple, and his hair was cropped close to his head. I'd shot him in his heart, and the entry wound was a silver-dollar-sized red spot. He lay in a growing pool of blood. It was also splattered on the bare walls.

I found a set of keys that included one for the padlock as well the ignition key for a Toyota truck. Blue growled and I paused as I crossed the room to Mujada's cage.

Blue was at the door, and I approached the window, crouching low. Shifting the curtain slightly, I looked out onto the road.

There were three men coming. Two dragged a body between them while the third formed a triangle behind them, rifles up. The prisoner's head hung loose between her shoulders, a dark ponytail bouncing back and forth, and her feet dragged on the ground. It was Zerzan.

Glancing around the room quickly, I noticed that there were two other cages and realized that they were probably coming this way. I pulled closed the curtain. Blue stood next to me as I planted my feet in a puddle of blood, my rifle at my shoulder, and knees slightly bent. I faced the door.

My entire body vibrated with adrenaline. I was seriously outnumbered, but I had plenty of rounds and a narrow opening that they would need to pass through to get me.

I heard them stop outside the door. They yelled, presumably asking the men I'd killed to open the door for them.

They spoke to each other. They knew something was wrong. I waited, figuring they'd need to investigate eventually. Blue released a very low growl that only I could hear, and a moment later the window shattered and a silver canister hit the floor.

It was to my left, and Blue was to my right. I dove, knocking Blue to the ground under me as a white light exploded.

EK

I squeezed my eyes shut, but the flash of light penetrated my closed lids.

The moment it was over, I was back on my feet, crouching down, rifle aimed at the door. White smoke billowed in the room, and my vision was spotted with bright lights.

My throat closed and my eyes stung as I recognized the burn of tear gas. Part of Joyful Justice training included exposure to the toxic smoke.

I coughed and Blue choked. In Mujada's weakened condition, this could kill her.

I picked up a chair and hurled it through the already broken window hoping to create a bigger hole. Glass shattered and the wooden chair became lodged in the frame, tear gas pouring out around it. I shoved Mujada's cage, pushing her into a corner, moving her out of direct line with the door.

Pushing my rifle onto my back, I pulled out my pistol. Motioning for Blue to stay behind me, I threw back the dead bolt and pulled the door open, staying behind it. White smoke whooshed out.

I'd expected a barrage of bullets.

There was only silence.

Smoke filled the doorway, billowing out onto the street. My vision was narrowing. Lowering myself to the ground, I peered around the edge of the door.

Through the smoke and my foggy vision, I saw several bodies on the ground. There was one figure standing. As the smoke lifted and shifted in the wind, I saw a bloody knife in her hand.

My vision darkened at the edges.

Zerzan's face and body were splattered with blood.

I crawled through the door. Zerzan grabbed my arm and helped me down the street as coughing seized me. She dropped me and I lay on my stomach coughing into the ground, dust rising up into my face. Blue lay down next to me, sneezing and coughing and crying. I rolled onto my back. Blue was on his stomach, pawing at his face. We needed water, and we needed it now.

I rose up on my knees and stumbled onto my feet, taking a couple of unsteady steps. White smoke was still spewing out of the open doorway, and tear gas was thick in the air.

Zerzan emerged from the doorway, a shirt wrapped around her head. She was hunched over as she dragged Mujada's cage.

"Stay!" I told Blue before jogging back down the road toward Zerzan. As the stronger plumes of tear gas hit me, my coughing became worse, but I continued forward. I pulled out the keys and handed them to Zerzan. She was coughing and tears streaked her face. She unlocked the padlock.

It sprang free and Zerzan pulled it loose, dropping it on the ground.

She tore open the cage door and reached in, grabbing Mujada under her arms. Mujada's body shook with a rasping cough.

I helped Zerzan, holding Mujada under the armpits while Zerzan pulled her legs free. We stumbled down the street toward Blue, and kept going until we reached the next building, where Zerzan directed us toward a door.

Luckily it was unlocked and the hallway was empty.

"There is a bathroom at the end of the hall," Zerzan said, her voice hoarse.

I turned on the shower, and we placed Mujada under the spray.

Zerzan stayed with her as I stumbled to the next shower stall. Blue had followed us, coughing and choking. His eyes were terribly red.

I turned on the shower, and Blue walked into it, lifting his face to the spray. My vision flickered, the scene turning black and white, like an old TV. I fell back, startled and frightened. My lower back hit against a sink, and I turned to it, throwing open both faucets. Cupping water in my hands, I held it to my eyes. Lightning seared across my closed lids, burning my eyes.

I coughed and water sprayed off my lips.

Thunder pounded in my head as I took shuddering breaths.

I looked back at Zerzan, Mujada and Blue. "How is she?" I asked.

"She is alive."

Blue stood in the shower, his eyes closed as water ran over his face. His breathing had regulated, but he was still coughing sporadically, his flanks shaking with the effort.

Mujada lay slumped in the shower, the spray hitting the back of her head; the water pooling around her was pink.

Zerzan's eyes were red and swollen; her cough had diminished to a slight rasp in her breath. I sat down next to her on the wet floor. She had a bruise on her temple and blood splattered her clothing.

"What happened?" I asked. Zerzan raised her eyebrows. "How did you kill three armed men?"

Zerzan's mouth twitched into a small smile. "They let me."

"They *let* you?"

"Yes, in that confused moment when they realized something had gone very wrong in the prison building, they dropped me in the dust to begin their assault on you. I was then free to come up behind them, one by one, and cut their throats. Not even the last one managed to utter a sound.

"Would they have done that with a male prisoner? I think not. So yes, they let me take their lives."

"What about Erzo, Dilsoz, and Hedar?"

"They're waiting for our direction."

Zerzan pulled her walkie-talkie off her belt and spoke into it. A reply came and she responded again.

"They will create a distraction so that we can escape. We will steal a vehicle and go out one of the two gated entrances."

"You've lost your weapons?"

"Everything but my knife."

I stood up, swaying slightly as I experienced lightheadedness from the quick movement. My breathing was returning to normal, but it was still labored, and each breath burned. When I blinked it felt like there was a layer of liquid fire on my eyes. The skin around my eyes was swollen and tight, my vision still cloudy at the edges.

Blue was breathing more easily. He stood under the spray, and I let him for a moment longer before turning off the shower.

He shook himself, spraying water everywhere.

I grabbed a small, white towel off a rack; it was still damp from the last person who had used it.

Zerzan turned off the shower over Mujada and used the towel to pat her dry. Then she draped the towel over Mujada's body and we picked her up. Mujada's head was slack on her neck, falling from side to side as we walked.

As we approached the exit of the building, we heard a massive explosion. There was yelling and gun blasts. Another explosion shook the building. Dust drifted down from the ceiling.

Using my leg to support Mujada, I took one hand off her and opened the door. Blue whined and I realized that he could not smell. His ears swiveled and he whined again.

With the explosions and gunfire and yelling, it was hard to tell if there was anyone outside.

Holding Mujada with my left arm, I used my right to pull my pistol. Keeping Mujada on my left side, I kicked the door open with my right foot. The street was empty.

I led the way, Zerzan directing me. A pickup truck barreled across the intersection in front of us, and my heart crashed against my ribs. The engine continued to roar, growing fainter as they continued toward the explosion. They had not noticed us.

We were moving too slowly. Zerzan held Mujada under her knees with her left arm, in her right hand she gripped my spare pistol.

Zerzan directed me to turn left and I followed her command. There was smoke in the air, and the sound of gunfire was growing closer. "The motor pool is right up ahead."

We reached the end of the building we were walking along, and I turned right to see a large parking lot and a small building. It was a smaller copy of the one at the base we'd recently escaped from.

Another explosion shook the ground. Lightning sizzled across my vision. I was losing it.

CHAPTER FOURTEEN

Smoke was thick in the air, along with dust from the damaged buildings and the lingering molecules of the gas. I was still coughing and tears were leaking out of my eyes. My vision was foggy and filled with hallucinations, the smoke turning to storm clouds, the gunfire to bolts of lightning, the hum of motors the prelude to thunder.

I focused on what was real— Mujada in my left hand, a pistol in my right.

We stopped at the first vehicle in the lot, a Toyota pickup truck. It was unlocked, but there were no keys. "Let's put her in and then I'll go find the keys," Zerzan said.

Shifting around, I stuck my gun into its holster then climbed into the truck, dragging Mujada into the passenger seat with me. I scooted across so that I was sitting in the open middle, Mujada in the seat. Zerzan pushed Mujada's legs into the footwell and slammed the door. Blue stood outside the truck, his ears perked in the direction of the gun battle.

I watched Zerzan through the dusty windshield as she ran over to the small building and ducked inside. Mujada was unconscious, but breathing. The towel pooled around her hips. Mujada's head rested against my shoulder and her long, matted hair fell over her face. I had an arm around her, and she was cuddled into my side.

Nausea tingled my jaw as I looked over her wounds; deep bruising, burns, and whip lashes. The cuts on her back looked rawer now that they were wet. I pulled my arm out from underneath her; my sleeve was soaked in blood. Would Mujada survive? And if she did, how different would she be? Would the torture make her stronger or destroy her?

The doors of the motor pool opened and Zerzan ran out and climbed into the driver's seat. Blue hopped into the bed of the pickup and laid flat, invisible to anyone on the ground. Zerzan shoved a key into the ignition and started the truck. She pulled out of the parking spot and shifted gears, speeding toward the exit.

As we raced down the deserted street, the sound of gunfire was getting louder with every second. I pulled my pistol out and Zerzan rolled down the window next to Mujada. I didn't want to move the injured woman, thinking about her wounds on the rough fabric of the seats, but at the same time, I knew I needed to have access to the window in order to defend us. I leaned across, and she slumped down once my shoulder was no longer propping her up. I pulled a grenade from my waist and kept it in my palm, waiting for the opportunity to use it.

Up ahead, we saw the exit and the battle waging.

Flames engulfed the guardhouse—licking toward the sky, hungry tongues of destruction. About thirty soldiers stood at the gate firing into the woods. "We won't get through," I said. Zerzan took a sharp left, and we almost collided with a pickup truck filled with more men.

Zerzan swerved around it, and I saw the shocked expression of three men in the front seat. They recovered quickly and pulled a U-turn to follow us. I climbed over Mujada's body and stuck my head and arms out the window as Zerzan sped toward the west gate.

I pulled the pin of the grenade with my teeth— the taste of metal filling my mouth. There was a mounted machine gun in the back of the pickup that was chasing us. A soldier wearing all black, including a headscarf, stood behind it. I underhanded the grenade at him.

His eyes widened as the grenade arced through the air. He took his hands off the weapon to try to deflect the projectile. The truck hit a pothole and jerked him off balance. He wobbled and then fell, the grenade following him down.

The man popped back up, the grenade in his hand. He threw it away but it ignited. The explosion was a cloud of fire and a shattering of noise. The man's hand and forearm evaporated. He screamed and fell again, this time over the edge of the truck and into the road. His body disappeared from my vision in the cloud of dust kicked up by the vehicle, which somehow kept going, despite the damage it sustained from the blast.

"Hold on!" Zerzan yelled.

The west gate was in front of us. There were four soldiers still guarding it. I fired at them, my aim thrown off by the jerking motion of the truck. They ducked down behind sandbag barricades but kept their weapons up, firing at the truck. Bullets exploded the headlights, thunked into the grill, and cracked the windshield.

I ducked back into the truck as Zerzan slammed on the gas and crashed through the closed metal gate. It exploded off its track and flew out of our way. The road was rough and we bounced over it as more bullets hit the back of the pickup.

We raced around a bend in the road and my shoulder slammed into the door. I pushed myself up and looked out the back. The pickup was still right behind us.

I checked on Blue. He was flat in the bed of the truck; his eyes found mine. They were red-rimmed from the tear gas, but other than that, he appeared uninjured.

The pickup was closing the distance between us. I grabbed another grenade. The soldier in the passenger seat leaned out his window, aiming a pistol at us.

I pushed myself through the window again. The soldier's trigger finger pulled back but I felt no fear. The man was afraid of me. I was a woman and I was powerful and that was a mix of impossible and terrifying to him. I knew what he was thinking. I heard it in the rumble of the thunder that radiated around us and I saw it in the lightning that branched out from the clouds that gathered on the edge of my vision.

His bullets went wide, cutting through the forest rather than into our truck. I took a deep breath as we jostled over the rough road and tossed the grenade. It arced over the windshield.

The soldier's eyes followed the trajectory of the sphere.

The driver slammed on the brakes and opened his door, diving out of the vehicle.

The grenade landed in the bed, by the foot of the unmanned machine gun.

The passenger fell out his door and scrambled away, leaving just the man in the middle. He tried to get out, throwing himself across the seats, reaching for the open door, but the grenade ignited before he made it.

A rush of orange flames and black smoke engulfed the vehicle. The road curved and I lost sight of the carnage, but the black smoke followed us around the bend.

CHAPTER FIFTEEN

Zerzan kept one hand on the wheel as she pulled her walkie-talkie out. She spoke into the device and received a response. I propped Mujada up again and sat back into my seat.

Checking on Blue, I found him in the same position. He locked gazes with me and I nodded; he blinked several times and then closed his eyes. The wind ruffled his fur. I scanned his body and the bed of the pickup truck: no blood. He was not hit.

Zerzan put her walkie-talkie back onto her waist.

"Everyone okay?" I asked.

"Yes," Zerzan replied. "They will return to the other truck."

"Won't they be followed?"

"Possibly. But they will be fine."

"How can you be so sure?"

"Faith." I had no response to that so I didn't speak.

"How is Mujada doing?" Zerzan asked.

She was still breathing. I placed two fingers on her throat and felt a heartbeat; the thumping of life, the pounding of thunder, the pattering of rain. "She's alive, but unconscious."

"It is best that she is not awake. She must be in much pain"

It was the first time I'd heard emotion in Zerzan's voice. There was a connection between these two. Was it just that they had fought together, or was there something more?

"Where are we going?"

"We need to get her to a doctor."

"Your grandfather?"

"I think she needs a better equipped facility."

"Then where are we going?"

"I am going to return to the base. They have the best medical facility, and I think that she will die without their help."

"The major will have you locked up."

"Yes; I will drop you off somewhere."

"Where would you drop me off? I don't speak the language, I don't know the area, I'm being hunted by Daesh, and the US government: where do you think I would be safe?"

Zerzan took her eyes off the road for a moment and looked at me. "You'd be safe anywhere. You and Blue are indestructible."

It started as a giggle but turned into a full-on belly laugh. My sides ached and fresh tears stung my eyes. "Then I guess we might as well come with you."

"If you want to."

I laughed again and swiped at the tears. "I like you, Zerzan. I really do."

"I like you too, Sydney."

We drove all night. I fell asleep, my head leaning back against the headrest, jaw hanging open. It was a restless sleep and I woke often, my mouth dry and the dark road still stretching out in front of us. Then I'd drift back to sleep. I was like a buoy in the ocean, diving under waves and then rising over them. The exhaustion was pulling me down and I let it. After the surge of adrenaline and battle, my body and mind needed the rest.

We stopped for gas, a small station manned by a young boy. Zerzan purchased an extra container and secured it in the bed of the truck with Blue.

I woke up as the sun rose over the road in front of us. I recognized the mountains rising up around us. Zerzan's hands were loose on the wheel, her eyes steady on the road. "You must be exhausted."

Zerzan glanced over at me for a second before returning her gaze to the road. "I am tired. I hope that the bed in my cell is comfortable."

"What makes you think they will treat Mujada?"

"They will help."

"I hope you're right. Do you want me to drive for a while?"

"I'm fine. Thank you."

Checking on Blue, I saw that he was also awake and sitting up. His eyes were closed as he let the wind brush over his face. He looked content to enjoy the breeze. Isn't that one of the amazing things about dogs? Their ability to stay in the present.

"How much longer?"

"Thirty minutes."

"I guess we better enjoy our last half hour of freedom."

Mujada moaned. She was still leaning against my shoulder. I'd rearrange the towel to cover her and try to keep her warm, but she looked pale and gray. Her eyes fluttered, then opened. They were unfocused and closed again. She took a deep shuddering breath, groaned in pain, and then slipped back into unconsciousness.

"I hope she makes it," I said.

"She will," Zerzan replied.

"Faith?"

"Yes."

When we pulled up to the base, there were two soldiers at the guns on the wall and four guards flanked the gate. Zerzan slowed and came to a stop, putting the vehicle into park.

Zerzan put both hands out the window and made sure the soldiers could see they were empty before bringing one back inside to open the door. She kept her hands up as she stepped away from the protection of the truck and began to walk toward them.

She spoke in Kurdish. One of the soldiers replied. Zerzan dropped to her knees, her arm still raised. A guard approached her and pulled handcuffs off her belt. She locked Zerzan's arms behind her back and then stood her up.

"Come out with your hands up," Zerzan told me. "They won't shoot you as long as you don't present a danger to them."

I opened my door. Mujada slumped as my support left her. I lowered her down gently to the seat and then, keeping my hands in front of me, climbed out.

A guard was removing Zerzan's weapons. Her father's knife glinted in the sun when they pulled it free of her ankle holster.

I stepped forward and dropped to my knees. "Tell them about Blue and I'll have him come out."

Zerzan spoke in Kurdish and the woman who appeared to be in charge responded.

"Okay."

I called Blue and he leapt from the back. The soldiers stepped back and aimed their weapons at him.

Zerzan spoke quickly and everyone calmed down. A guard approached me and began to remove my weapons. I kept my hands in the air.

"Are they bringing someone for Mujada?"

"Yes, they've radioed to have the paramedics come."

Blue came closer to me but I told him to keep his distance. He looked rough, his eyes still red from the tear gas, his coat caked in dust from having been wet and then ridden all night in the back of a pickup truck.

"Tell them that Blue will come with me and he won't hurt anyone."

Zerzan spoke and the woman responded. "They won't let him inside."

Then I'm not going.

The leader spoke and Zerzan replied. They'd handcuffed me at this point and were hauling me to my feet when the gate opened and an ambulance came out. I stumbled and the soldier holding my arm loosened her grip. I coughed and put more weight against the soldier's grasp, trying to fall to the ground again.

I just needed to buy a few more minutes. The soldier let go of me, allowing me to hit the road rather than be dragged down with me. She aimed her rifle at me and yelled something. "She says you have to get up."

I didn't respond. I just continued to cough. It wasn't hard considering the state of my lungs. They felt raw and the coughing scratched a painful inch.

The leader said something to Zerzan, who responded. I watched as the ambulance approached the truck and two women jumped out, hurrying to the passenger side opening. I eased up my coughing and took some steadying breaths, continuing to lie on the ground, my arms handcuffed behind me and my head resting on the sandy pavement.

The paramedics maneuvered Mujada onto a stretcher. The towel fell away from her body and her wounds were exposed to the bright light of day.

The night in the truck had not improved them. The welts were puffier and redder. The bruises darker. The blisters on the burns had popped and yellow, raised sores dotted her body.

I kept breathing, regaining my strength as the paramedics loaded her into the ambulance. I began to stand up as they closed the doors and the driver ran around to climb back into their seat. The soldier grabbed my arm and finished pulling me up. I followed her toward the open gate.

The ambulance went through it and then Zerzan and her soldier followed. I was about to walk through when Blue barked a warning. I suddenly decided that coming back to the base was a very bad idea.

I dropped low, wrenching myself free from the guard. I spun on my left foot and lashed out with my right, bringing the soldier to the ground. I rolled backwards bringing my cuffed hands over my feet to the front of my body.

I lunged and grabbed the side arm off the soldier who'd been escorting me inside and held it on her. She stared at me with wide eyes. It had happened quickly, but the other soldiers noticed.

I yanked the guard by the arm with my free hand and pulled her body in front of mine as I duck-walked backwards.

I held her by the hair at the base of her head, the pistol pressed against the back of her skull.

The remaining guards all aimed their weapons at me.

"Truck, Blue," I yelled. His nails tinged against the metal as he jumped back into the bed of the pickup.

I continued moving backwards. The guard's helmet fell forward and covered her eyes. Zerzan was on her knees, a pistol to her head. Her face was unlined and her expression serene. The gun muzzle pressing against her temple was digging into her flesh.

The leader was yelling. I couldn't understand a word.

I maneuvered to the open driver side door. Keeping the soldier's body in front of me I pressed my back up against the seat and then stepped up into the vehicle. I was exposed for a moment but none of them took the shot. I pulled the woman in after me so that she was sitting in the driver seat and I was in the middle. I stayed low, pressing the gun into the woman's stomach.

The truck was still on and I told her to put it in gear. The soldier looked down at me, her eyebrows knitted together. She had big, brown eyes and pink gloss on her lips.

I gestured with my chin toward the gear shift. "Back it up." She reached for the shifter, putting the truck into reverse. "Faster." She didn't increase her speed so I used my elbows to press down on her leg.

The truck sped up. The doors of the truck were still open and wind rushed into the cab.

I lifted my head. We were a good distance from the front gate. Zerzan was still on her knees. The other soldiers were yelling and waving at each other. They'd be following us soon.

I held up my bound wrists, the gun still on her. My captive took a hand off the wheel and pulled a key out from her pocket. She slowed down and nearly came to a stop as she used one hand to unlock my cuffs.

Once I was free I told her to stop. She understood that one. I gestured for her to get out. She didn't pause before launching herself out the open door. I shifted into her seat, threw the truck into gear, and with both doors still open, did a U-turn; that bounced me off the pavement into the sandy shoulder and then back up onto the road. I hit the gas to the floor and the truck jerked forward. I quickly shifted through the gears until we were in fifth, flying down the road. The doors slammed shut as my speed increased. I checked the rearview and saw through the cloud of dust that we were being followed.

A convoy of vehicles was exiting the compound. As we reached the first twist in the road and I went around the bend, I lost sight of them. Scanning the road ahead, I saw dirt tracks leading off of it.

I knew I was headed in the direction of Zerzan's territory. It was safer than going toward Daesh-controlled land, but at this point there was no mercy for us. I needed to call Dan. I hoped that he, with the help of our connections, could get me out of there.

I took the third dirt track to the left. The shocks on the truck struggled to keep the frame from bouncing right off the wheels.

The road continued for several miles and I went as fast as the truck allowed. It dead-ended at a burnt-out house. Next to the house was a burnt-out truck. "Shit."

I parked the pickup next to the burnt one and climbed out of the vehicle. There were some supplies in the bed and I pulled out a couple bottles of water.

Blue followed me as I hiked into the cover of the trees. We continued for forty-five minutes until I could no longer see the destroyed home or anything except for forest.

It was rough going, there was no trail, and the undergrowth was thick. If they found the truck, we would be easy to follow into the woods. However, I didn't know why they would bother.

I still had Mary's comm device in my jacket pocket and I pulled it out, hoping Dan was monitoring the line. Turning it on, I listened to static for a moment before speaking. "Are you there?"

There was no response. I drank some, then tipped the bottle and Blue lapped at the water that spilled out.

I sat down on a fallen tree and listened to the static in my ear as the day waned. Blue sat next to me and then eventually lay down and closed his eyes. There were no sounds but the ones associated with nature: birds and breeze and shuffling of little legs through fallen leaves.

The lightning and thunder in my mind were silent for the moment. But I sensed them lurking right over the horizon. This was just the calm before the storm.

I tried reaching out to Dan every hour or so. He didn't respond until the forest was growing dark, the shadows taking over. My hunger had abated and was replaced with a slight nausea when finally I heard his voice. "Sydney?"

"I'm ready to get out of here."

"We've got a plan in place. You need to get to where I can land a helicopter."

I laughed. "Sure," I said looking around at the forest. "I'll get right to the closest helipad."

Dan ignored my sarcasm.

"There's a spot about fifteen miles from where you are. It's a plateau. You're gonna have a hell of a hike to get there."

"Any way you can airdrop me a sandwich?"

Dan laughed. "Sorry, I'll have the team bring some food with them."

"Tell me what I need to do."

Dan gave me directions and I memorized them. I still had my compass, so I was somewhat prepared. I figured I had just about enough water. But carrying it without a pack was a pain in the ass.

I began my hike immediately, but when the sun set and the forest became pitch black, I kept tripping. Blue touched my hip and whined softly, indicating that I was acting a fool. I had no choice but to stop for the night.

At the first light of dawn, we were both up and moving. The hike was steep and without a machete, the underbrush was a difficult obstacle. I let Blue lead sometimes and others I would go ahead. We were only about three miles from our destination when I saw something gray up ahead.

A cliff.

We reached the base of the cliff and I stood there, staring up at it. The height of a three-story building, it stretched horizontally for as far as I could see in either direction. I sat down on one of the large, gray rocks that had fallen off the face and opened the communication line. There was a woman waiting for me, and when I explained the situation, she was silent for a moment. I could hear a clicking keyboard. "Oh yeah, I see that."

I refrained from saying something sarcastic.

"Looks like if you head southeast for about five miles, you come to a more gradual approach."

There was nothing to do but continue and so, checking my compass, Blue and I headed off. At least there wasn't much underbrush as we followed the cliff line and I still had water. "Look at me, looking at the bright side," I said to Blue.

He stopped and raised his head, flexing his nostrils. I stopped and watched him. He released a low growl. He continued to sniff the air and then took a step forward before glancing up at me. I watched him closely. His hackles rose and adrenaline released into my veins.

I pulled out my pistol. The forest was to our left, the cliffs to our right. Up ahead were more trees and more cliff. I scanned the trees, seeing only the play of light and dark between the branches.

I examined the cliff side. A darkening indicated a cave. Fighters?

Blue stepped toward the forest and I followed him. We worked through the thick underbrush until we were about thirty feet back from the cliffs. We could still see the gray of the stone, but it was hard to make out details through the thick foliage.

We walked parallel to the cliff, our progress slow and noisy. It took us about fifteen minutes to come even with the site of the cave. I could see through the brush that the opening was about ten feet wide by seven feet tall. Sunlight did not penetrate the space.

Blue sniffed the air again, and I began to continue our path through the brush, but he stopped me with a low whine. I looked back at him and then the cave. He sat and continued to stare at the opening, his nostrils pumping. I sniffed the air trying to find the scent he was on to. Closing my eyes, I picked up the smell of cooking meat. As soon as I smelled it, it amplified and my mouth began to water.

There was someone in that cave cooking some kind of meat. Blue wanted it, and so did I. But since we had no idea who was in the cave, it seemed supremely stupid to go after it.

From what I understood of the local geography, we were in Kurdish land. So theoretically, the soldiers in that cave, or whoever they were, should be somewhat friendly. They at least wouldn't automatically want to enslave me.

But there was no way of knowing for sure.

Blue touched his nose to my hip and looked back at the cave. "No boy," I whispered. As I began to walk away, he followed, but also let out an exasperated sigh. "Sorry. I'm hungry too."

We hiked through the underbrush for another fifteen minutes before I felt it was safe to return to the cliff side. Our progress was much quicker, and we reached the gentler incline we'd been promised.

I began to climb up, grabbing onto tree branches.

Blue bounded ahead, waiting every ten to twenty feet or so. Bracing himself against the hillside, he'd look back down at my slow progress. Occasionally, he would loosen rocks, which tumbled down onto me.

"Blue, stay." He waited for me, and when I reached him, I told him to stay again before continuing on. Of course, then I was knocking rocks down onto him and he barked in protest. "Okay, fine."

Blue bounded up next to me, his tongue lolling out of his head, and then ran past.

At the top, I sat down to rest, drinking the last of my water. I'd filled one of the empty bottles with stream water and gave some to Blue.

It was another two hours of hiking through thick foliage by the time we reached the plateau where the helicopter could land. I lay down in the fragrant grass and opened the comm unit again.

My mouth was dry and I felt dehydration starting to mix with hunger into a dangerous cocktail of exhaustion and lethargy.

Dan answered and I let him know that I was in place. "A team will be with you in six hours."

I stifled a groan.

We got off the line and I closed my eyes. It was around four o'clock and the sun was just dipping behind the trees. I laid my jacket out flat and put my weapons around me before lying down, planning on taking a nap. Blue lay down next to me and closed his eyes, but his ears swiveled, searching for danger.

I fell asleep to the melody of the forest in late afternoon.

I woke up to Blue standing over me, growling. The moon was up, bathing the plateau in pale silver light.

I listened to the night and heard bugs chirping, the wind blowing through the pines, and Blue's warning growl again. He was looking back into the forest, which was pure blackness to me.

My pistol in hand, the safety clicked off, I stayed still, reserving my strength and listening. There was shuffling in the woods. Some kind of animal was out there. Was it human?

The people in the cave could be out doing rounds. Or it could be a bear, fox, anything big enough to make that kind of noise.

Blue looked up toward the sky and moments later I heard that chop of helicopter blades in the air. The rescue team was here, but if there were armed men in the forest, then we might have a problem.

Blue returned his attention to the woods, his hackles rising. The shuffling was getting closer. "Down."

Blue lowered himself slowly, his growl maintaining its low warning hum.

"Quiet." He cut off the sound.

The helicopter was getting closer—as were the footsteps. They were definitely human. Perhaps two or three people. What could I do? There was no way of knowing who was in the woods.

If they were Daesh, then they would almost certainly engage. If they were just random people living in these woods in order to escape the war, then hopefully they would bugger off. The helicopter noise grew and then it was above us.

I could no longer hear the movements from the forest. I had no way of warning the helicopter that there were others on the ground.

I just had to have faith they would not engage.

The helicopter landed, throwing up dust, its wind pushing at my hair. Keeping my pistol in my hand I crawled across the grass toward the helicopter.

Two men jumped out. They were huge: bulging arms, wide shoulders, and narrow waists. They moved away from the helicopter, one in each direction. I waited until one of them was about fifteen feet away before making my presence known.

"I'm over here. There are others in the woods. I don't know how many."

I continued crawling toward him. The man shifted his attention toward us and pointed his rifle into the woods behind me.

I got on my hands and knees, then ran toward him in a crouch, Blue by my side. The man let me pass him and then moved backwards headed for the helicopter.

Blue and I jumped into the open helicopter and seconds later, the two men were on board as well. The doors remained open as I clicked myself into a seat and the helicopter began to rise.

EK

The earphones muffled the thwapping sound of the helicopter blades. When I was done with my sandwich, the solider who'd handed it to me took the wrappings and shoved them into a bag by his side. With the doors closed, the space warmed quickly and I felt at once tired and revived. The food was giving me energy, but also taking it away.

Blue sat next to me. I placed a hand on his back. His fur was snarled with twigs and pine needles.

"I am Terry," the man who'd taken my sandwich wrapping said. He touched the brim of his helmet in a small nod.

"Nice to meet you. I'm Sydney."

"We know." He smiled and pointing to the other man and said, "This is Avery."

"Thanks for the pickup." I smiled. "Where we headed to?"

"About two hours north, across the Turkish border, to a base run by Fortress Global Investigations."

"You're Fortress Global employees?"

"That's right. Most dangerous men alive."

"Don't I know it."

I stared out into the night; a smattering of clouds hung at the horizon, dark smudges of matte black against a background of smooth velvet.

Bobby Maxim had run quite a number on Fortress Global Investigations, the company he founded and ran before taking it public, dumping all his stock, and nearly tanking it. He got out rich, even richer than he already was, which was already filthy rich.

These guys picking me up meant he still had pull within his former organization. Hopefully he was still on my side. Our relationship was complicated and while I'd spent years hating him for stealing my revenge—he killed Kurt Jessup before I could—recently we'd reached an accord. He'd saved my life on a number of occasions, which really does help build trust.

The helicopter blades spun slowly above us as we climbed out of the bird. Avery escorted me across the tarmac. We passed several other helicopters, and I could see jets and large transport planes dotted around the airfield. Avery opened the door to a low-slung building.

Inside looked like any other office building in America. A waiting room with gray wall-to-wall carpeting, a couch and two chairs, their upholstery scratchy but stain resistant.

A woman wearing black fatigues with her blonde hair up in a high ponytail that poked out the back of her black baseball cap sat behind a wooden desk. She smiled when she saw Avery. "Hey there."

"Samantha, this is Sydney."

"Oh yeah." She smiled and nodded. "They're waiting for you."

Blue's nose tapped my hip and I laid a hand on his head.

Samantha came around her desk and moved toward the only other door in the room. She knocked once and then opened it. "Sydney is here."

"Great."

I recognized Bobby's voice. He was supposed to be on a beach somewhere enjoying his retirement and occasionally helping out Joyful Justice, but I wasn't surprised that he was less than honest about his whereabouts or plans.

I rolled my shoulders back before entering the office.

When Blue saw Bobby, his tail wagged, smacking into my butt as it went. Maxim was standing by a large desk. He was wearing the same black fatigues as all the other staff; on the left breast was FGI's emblem. The globe with rings around it...like, *we got all this covered.*

"Bobby, what a surprise," I said with sarcasm dripping from each word.

"You know I can't stay away, sweetheart." He stepped forward and took my elbow, leaning down to kiss my cheek.

He smelled like sandalwood soap. His brown hair, graying at the temples, was pushed back from his face. His eyes sparkled, shifting colors; the guy was a real chameleon.

"Allow me to introduce you to some of my dearest friends." Bobby turned to the two other people in the room. A woman in her sixties and a man around the same age.

The woman looked familiar, but I couldn't place her. She had sharp green eyes behind large glasses. Her hair was blonde with streaks of silver and short, brushed back off of her face in a style that made it look like she was walking into a stiff wind. Her clothing was more formal: a business suit in olive green with rounded lapels, like, *I'm a badass, but also have a softer side.* I didn't believe her lapels.

"This is Martha Emerson. She's the director of the CIA."

Holy fuck.

She was sitting behind the desk and didn't stand, just gave a small nod. "And this," Bobby said pointing to the man standing next to her, "is Patrick Larson, her deputy."

"Nice to meet you both. I think. What's up?"

"Well," Bobby said, stepping deeper into the room, keeping his hand on my elbow, pulling me in. "We heard about Mary's little program. Declan's cancellation of it. You shooting him." He raised his eyebrows at me. I shrugged. He smiled, his eyes twinkling. "Then you came back with an injured woman whom you rescued from a Daesh compound, basically destroying it in the process."

"I know how I spent the last week, Bobby. What I don't know is what you all want from me."

"Have a seat." Martha said, gesturing with her chin at one of the chairs facing her desk.

"Why don't we all sit down," Bobby said, waving for Patrick to sit and letting go of my elbow. Bobby pulled up another chair for himself, making a nice little circle, and sat first, putting his hands on the armrests and looked up at us expectantly.

Patrick and I both sat slowly. Blue stood next to me, his large head above the armrest of the chair, staring across the desk at Martha. "Okay, I'm sitting. What's up?"

"The program that Mary was working on," Martha said. "I think it has legs. And I want to continue it."

"Okay," I said. "You could have saved us all a lot of time and effort if you'd decided that like three days ago."

"Could have saved Declan surgery," Bobby said with a smile.

"Anyway," I continued. "I think it's smart and I don't understand why it was cancelled. But I don't understand the politics around what you people do."

"You people?" Martha said. "You think you're not one of us?"

Lightning sizzled in the corner of the room, the electric charge raising the hairs on my arms. "I'm positive I'm not one of you." *Unless we can all see that storm cloud brewing over the filing cabinet.*

"I thought you were more self-aware."

"Considering we've never met before, it'd be hard for you to know anything about me, wouldn't it?"

Martha was staring at me, her eyes bright and calculating. "I'm not interested in arguing with you."

"Look, you want to continue what Mary started. I think that's a great idea. A good first step would be meeting with Zerzan. She's really the person you to need to talk to. I just spent several days on the run, so I'm tired, and I'd kill for a shower. Blue needs a bath. And I'm not so sure that I can trust you or vouch for you with Zerzan."

"You trusted Mary?"

"I thought she was genuine in what she wanted to do."

"And you don't think I'm genuine?" Martha smiled; she reminded me quite strikingly of a snake.

"I don't know you. I know that there are lots of moving parts here that I'm not aware of. I don't know why this program would be so controversial. Seems to me you're arming all sorts of groups to fight

Daesh. Arming these women, helping them in every way we possibly can, that seems like a no-brainer to me."

"*We?*"

"I misspoke. I meant, you."

"Is Joyful Justice helping them?"

"No. If you'll recall I'd never even heard of these people until you guys brought me—"

"Homeland Security brought you in," Patrick interrupted. "We're CIA."

"Great. I'm happy for you. My point is that this isn't my show. I'm here because Mary Leventhal blackmailed me into coming."

"You shot Declan Doyle," Bobby interjected. I looked over at him, he was smiling again.

"Yes, I shot him. But I specifically tried not to kill him."

Bobby laughed and shook his head. "Martha, Sydney obviously wants to help. The only reason she shot Declan is because he threatened to lock her up. I bet she would do the same to any one of us."

Martha's lip twitched. "Do you think Zerzan will be a problem?"

"Zerzan is incredible. I've never seen anyone fight like her, and I see a lot of really good fighters. The woman is an inspiration. I think that she would have no trouble recruiting new people to the cause. I think she just needs money, guns, and maybe some training for troops."

"She suffered quite a loss in that Russian drone attack."

"So did we," Patrick said.

"Both sides did," I said. "Right before that happened, though, we were getting somewhere. I know that Zerzan was willing to talk. I'm guessing she still is. I'm not sure what the problem is."

"We think Mary made a vital mistake," Patrick said. Wasn't he just Mr. Talkative now.

"Which was?"

"Bringing you in."

"I'm happy to leave. That was my plan." I looked over at Bobby. "I assume I'm free to go?"

"Of course, darling. I'm happy to take you home at any time."

Martha sat forward, leaning her elbows on the desk. "Don't make promises you can't keep, Bobby."

"I always keep my promises." It was a statement, but it sounded an awful lot like a threat.

"What do you want?" I asked Martha.

"We want Zerzan to share information with us."

"Then you should talk to her. She was on the verge of agreeing to work with Mary at the time of the drone attack, and after Mary was killed, she was still ready to negotiate with whoever was left in charge. So I don't see a problem here. If you want I can talk to her."

"The problem is that you've been involved," Bobby said. "Joyful Justice, as you know, is a terrorist organization. Zerzan's organization is also considered a terrorist organization, and the US can't be seen as supporting terrorists. So, the path forward for Martha and Patrick is either to remove Zerzan's organization from the terrorist list, which would raise a lot of questions in Washington, or to convince her to start a new organization without all the baggage."

"Okay."

"The thing is, they want to do the same thing for Joyful Justice."

"What do you mean?"

"We want Joyful Justice to disappear, and we want you to become something else," Martha said.

"This all sounds insane." I laughed. "What we're talking about here is figuring out how to get weapons and support to an all-female fighting force to help defeat our common enemy: Daesh. Names strike me as rather irrelevant."

"We call them ISIS."

"And that proves my point."

"Names are very powerful," Martha said, her voice low. "Certain organizations—think of the KKK in the US—are beyond redemption in our view."

"That's your problem."

"Yes, and you're the one who has a solution."

"Fine, I am no longer a member of Joyful Justice. Happy now?"

Patrick made a small noise in his throat. Martha sat back in her chair and crossed her arms.

Bobby stood and I followed suit, Blue moving in close to my hip. "I'm taking Sydney back to my room so she can shower and we can talk."

Martha glared at him but didn't try to stop us as we left the room. Samantha was back behind her desk, and she nodded as we walked out. Bobby took my hand once we were on the tarmac and began to pull me along the side of the building toward another entrance about thirty feet away. "Let go of my hand!"

"Come now, Sydney. Trust me."

"Holding your hand is in some way important for that?"

"Don't worry, sweetheart. I've got a plan."

He opened the door and placed his hand on the small of my back, ushering me in first. "My room is down on the left." Bobby's hand was warm on my back and Blue stayed close to my hip, occasionally touching it with his nose.

Bobby opened the door to his room and gestured for me to enter. It was a huge, lavish space. The living room was filled with sumptuous furniture and a full-size dining table. There were tinted windows with mountain views. "Nice place."

"The bathroom is through there." Bobby gestured to an open doorway. I could see a king-sized bed. "I'll get you some new clothing. I think I'll be able to rustle up an FGI uniform." He smiled. "I always wanted to see you in one."

I brought Blue into the bathroom with me and locked the door. I trusted Bobby Maxim with my life, but not with an unlocked door that I was naked behind. I let my mind go blank as I peeled off the clothing I'd been wearing for days and got the shower going.

The bathroom was huge, all marble with a shower stall and a bathtub. Should I take a bath? Cleanse away the last few days, sink into the water, and let the tension release so that my mind could think?

No. There wasn't time.

Besides, slipping into a bath wasn't going to make the storm cloud hovering over my head, rumbling with thunder, disappear.

I stepped into the shower. The hot water made every scratch on me sting. My hike through the woods and days of rough treatment had taken a toll on my body. In addition to the small scrapes that littered my arms and legs, there were bruises on my hips, and my ankle was still discolored.

I closed my eyes and let the water flow over me, blocking out all sounds except the whoosh of liquid.

Changing names and wiping the slate clean was not without precedence in my life. I was Joy Humbolt, and am now Sydney Rye.

While I was not attached to the name Joyful Justice (I actually thought it was super cheesy and kind of hated it … just a little), I was attached to the people who made up the organization and the mission that it pursued. Changing the name would make it more difficult for people to find us, and therefore for us to help them. That felt like too big a price to pay. Why they couldn't just negotiate without me, letting Zerzan change the name of her group and going from there, I didn't know.

Clean and wrapped in a towel I tried to comb out my hair with one of the combs that had been wrapped in plastic and left on the vanity for people like me who traveled without such niceties.

My hair was knotted and I winced as I pulled the comb through it. There was a knock on the door. "I've got your clothing."

Blue stood by the door. I unlocked it and opened it a crack. Bobby was grinning. "You are ridiculously predictable," I said, taking the folded uniform from him. Bobby opened his mouth to speak, but I closed the door and locked it again. "We can talk once I'm dressed."

"Okay."

The black uniform Bobby had given me fit well enough. It had the Fortress Global Investigations insignia on the left breast and I stared at the thing for a moment. The name that one fought under was important. But how important?

I had concluded that changing my name or the name of Joyful Justice was unacceptable. Would Zerzan feel the same? Her situation was direr. And she was fighting for a more tangible outcome than I was.

Would the Tigress be less deadly by a different name—or fighting under a different banner?

Bobby was waiting for me in the bedroom. He was lying on the bed, his body propped up with pillows and his ankles crossed. He looked up from the book he was reading and smiled at me. I walked past him and out to the living room. He followed moments later. "So?" I said as I sat on the couch. Blue sat next to me, watching me closely.

"Feel better?"

"Come on, Maxim. What's going on here?"

"You always like to get straight to the point."

"And you always like dicking around."

He nodded and smiled again. "Simply put, I think we're in a very powerful position. You made a valuable connection. I have many valuable connections. What I suggest we do is start our own company."

"Excuse me?"

"The world is more dangerous than it's ever been." Bobby sat down in an armchair across from me. "There are terrorist groups springing up everywhere. Fortress Global Investigations, the most trusted organization in the field, has recently suffered a major setback."

"That you made happen."

"Yes. But that's not the point. The point is that there is an opening in the market. And you and I could fill it."

"Wait, you want to start a security company with me?"

"Yes. A lot of good men are losing their jobs. We've got the capital. We have influence with Joyful Justice, the FKP, and many other organizations. We'd be unstoppable."

I held up a hand. "Bobby, slow down. Are you insane?" I felt a little like the kettle calling out the pot, but still. "I'm not starting a for-profit company that's going to protect the kinds of people that Joyful Justice pursues. Jesus."

"But don't you see how much good you can do?"

"How much good I can do?"

"Yes, think about it Sydney. The US government needs a trustworthy company to work with on these kinds of sensitive missions. One that has connections that will help keep everything going smoothly."

"What about me makes you think I want to make sure things go smoothly for the US government?"

"With the amount of money we can make, we could arm Zerzan's group ourselves."

"Joyful Justice can do that. We have enough money. Bobby, I'm not going to start a for-profit, security-for-hire company with you to replace the one that you founded and destroyed. That's insane." A lightning bolt shot across the room, the thunder that followed so loud it almost drowned Bobby out.

"Sydney, I knew you'd have reservations."

I stood up and took a deep breath. "Reservations? Bobby I don't have reservations. I'm not doing it."

Bobby stood up; he was taller than me. But he wasn't trying to use his height to intimidate me. He was smiling, which made me want to punch him in his stupid face. "I understand that you don't want to do this. But if you want to avoid ending up in a black ops prison, then you have to. You have to start this company with me because it's going to legitimize you, which is going to make it possible for us," he put his hand over his own chest, "to get the contract to train Zerzan's people."

"You bastard."

"Look, I'm not the only one who thinks this is a good idea. Dan agrees with me."

"I'd want to hear that directly from him."

"That's not really safe here."

"Fuck!"

"Sure, happy to."

"Ugh, you're disgusting. Which is another reason I don't want to be partners with you."

"Come on, Sydney." Bobby stepped toward me, his hands out by his side, palms up. "This is brilliant. Don't you see? It gives Joyful Justice a legitimate arm. The kind of intel we would have! The resources!"

"Fortress Global Investigations represented people who Joyful Justice targeted. Wouldn't our new company also represent these sorts of people? The ones who have something to fear and can afford our services?"

"Here's how it would work. Let's say Joyful Justice has a problem with someone. What's the first thing you do?"

"We deliver a warning and a message of change. An outline of steps to take in order to avoid our wrath."

"Exactly. Now, who better to help them with that change than a company like the one you and I could create? We are going to do this right." He took another step closer to me, entering my personal space, which made Blue push against my side. "This is how we save the world."

I laughed. "You want to save the world?"

"Sydney, I've told you before. I'm a changed man. You inspire me." He was even closer now. I put my hand on his chest to stop him.

"Bobby, get the fuck out of my personal space." I pushed back.

He stumbled holding his hands to his chest. "You break my heart, darling."

"I'm not your darling. I hate that shit."

He smiled. "I love that you shot Declan Doyle."

"I can tell."

"This is the only way to do this," Bobby said and sat back down in the chair, his eyebrows raised. "They can't let you go if you're Sydney Rye, Joyful Justice council member and top operative."

"What was Mary going to do?"

"What Declan wanted to do: lock you up. First, of course, they were going to use you to the full extent that they could."

I smiled. "So Declan's plan wasn't to get shot?"

Bobby laughed. "This makes it all good. You won't be Sydney Rye of Joyful Justice. You'll be Sydney Rye, co-founder of...well, what would you want to call it?"

"I'm not doing this." I started to walk toward the door. Bobby jumped up and grabbed my arm. Blue let out a low warning growl. Bobby looked down at him, his gaze fierce. Blue locked eyes with Bobby, his hackles rising.

"You two always do this," I said.

"That's why he respects me," Bobby said, not taking his eyes from Blue's.

"Let go of me—and get me the fuck out of here."

"If I get you out of here, it will be bloody. And Zerzan will be left with no support."

"Joyful Justice will support her."

"You don't have the resources or know-how to operate in this war zone." Blue growled and Bobby growled back.

"Enough!"

Blue sat and licked his lips. Bobby turned his gaze to me, his hand still on my arm.

"You've been here for what? A week?" Bobby said. "You think you have any idea what is going on this region? It's a shit show. And you have no one on the ground."

"I have Zerzan."

"She can't get weapons in here. You have no way of moving supplies."

"We can figure it out."

"You don't even have a way of contacting Zerzan right now." He had points. Bobby-fucking-Maxim always seemed to have a point. "What I'm offering you is the best deal you're ever going to get."

"The best deal ever?"

"Your other option is that we leave. You and I fight our way out of here. There are men loyal to me here, we could do it. You know I've always got an escape plan. But, that doesn't get you what you want. You want to help Zerzan."

"I do."

"I know, and so does Dan. So do the rest of the Joyful Justice council members. That's why I'm here. That's why this offer is on the table. Because it makes sense. Because it's smart."

I couldn't believe it. Without talking to the other council members, it was impossible to know if Bobby had actually spoken to them. But agreeing to this while here seemed like my only option. If later I wanted to back out, I could. Bobby was smart and he was dangerous, but I'd evaded him before, and I could do it again.

"Fine."

"Fine? You'll do it? We'll be partners?"

"Partners? Blue's my partner. You're, well, you're whatever you are."

Bobby laughed. "I'm not sure we can get Blue's name on the incorporation papers, but we'll see."

"So, you can take your hand off me now." Bobby looked down at where his hand was clasped around my bicep.

"Or..." He pulled me and I moved an inch closer to him before yanking free of his hold.

"Ew, stop it. You can't sexually harass me in the first 30 seconds we're in business together."

Bobby shrugged. "Can't blame a guy for trying."

"Yes, you can. That's exactly what you can do. In fact, back in the real world, you can sue a guy for trying. So just stop."

Bobby put his hands up. "Fine, fine. Partner."

CHAPTER SIXTEEN

We returned to Martha's office to give her the good news. She smiled, or at least her lips curled. "And you think Zerzan will be willing to make a break from her old organization and start again?"

"I guess I'll have to ask her."

"That would be great."

Martha leaned forward and pressed a button on her phone "Samantha, can you take us to see Zerzan?"

"Sure thing, boss."

"She's here?"

"Yes." Martha nodded and leaned back in her chair. "Bobby assured me that we could make this work, so I had her brought here. She is in an interrogation room. I think it's a more suitable environment to have this discussion."

"Do you?"

"Come on, Sydney; let's go." Bobby said, taking my elbow.

Zerzan sat at a table, her hands cuffed. She looked tired but uninjured. Her face was that same blank mask that she used whenever trouble sprung up.

"I think you should talk to her," Martha said turning to me. "Explain that she needs to part ways with her old organization and then we can get whatever she needs."

"Sure. But I don't think all this is necessary. She's a completely reasonable person." Patrick laughed under his breath. "What?"

"You're talking about the leader of an all-female fighting force that has more kills to its name than any other Kurdish militia."

"And that person can't be reasonable?"

"That person could be reasonable. But that one," Patrick pointed through the glass, "isn't."

"Oh, you know her so well."

"I know enough." He turned to Martha. "You know my feelings on this project."

"Yes," Martha said not taking her eyes off Zerzan. "And if you try to express them again, I'll stop listening to any of your thoughts."

Patrick's face flushed.

I was starting to like Martha.

Zerzan looked up as Blue and I entered the room. She smiled. "You made it out alive." Her gaze fell to my hands. "And are still free?"

"Of course. You never doubted that, did you?"

Zerzan shrugged. "I guess not."

"And Mujada?" I tensed in anticipation of the answer.

"Her recovery will be slow, but she is receiving good care."

I took the seat across from her and looked over at the mirror, which I knew Martha, Patrick, and Bobby stood behind. "I cut a deal. I'm here to help you do the same."

Zerzan looked over at the mirror. "Is that right?"

"Yes. There are people who are interested in continuing what Mary started."

"Okay, then why am I in chains?" She held up her wrists and the cuffs jingled.

"They need you to start fresh, to disassociate yourself from the FKP."

Zerzan laughed. "And what do I get with this change of identity?"

"A whole lotta help. Money, weapons, whatever you need."

"And how is that going to happen?"

"I'll be the one delivering it to you."

Zerzan's eyebrows rose. "Joyful—"

I cut her off. "Dog Fight Investigations will be handling the logistics."

"So I'm not the only one with a new identity?"

"Something like that."

"Fine. Do they have a new name in mind for this new group I assemble?"

"Nah, they'll let you pick that." I smiled.

Zerzan laughed. "Great. Now can I get these cuffs off?" She held up her bound wrists. I looked over at the mirror and my own reflection.

A moment later the door opened again and Bobby and Martha entered. Bobby unlocked Zerzan's cuffs. She rubbed her wrists. "Thank you."

"You're very welcome."

"My name is Martha Emerson. I am glad to hear that you're willing to disassociate from the FKP."

"What matters is the cause I'm fighting for and that's not changing."

Martha did that spasm thing again with her lips that I was pretty sure was a smile. "I hope we can be friends." She sat down next to me. Martha smelled like soap and laundry detergent, with a whiff of aerosol hairspray. "We've spent a lot of time studying how ISIS attracts young men to join their organization. As you are aware, they are pulling disenfranchised youth from all over Europe. And, of course, the Middle East."

"Yes, I know," Zerzan said. She was watching Martha closely, her eyes narrowed.

"They even posted a video claiming to have killed you."

"I know that. But as you can see, I'm alive."

"Yes, of course. But I think that you've hidden yourself too well."

"You think that I should come out and deny the video?"

"I think we can do better than that," Bobby said.

I recognized the glint in his eye. This scheme was going to be epic.

"The man who made the video, Abu Mohammad al-Baghdadi. We know where he is. And we think with the right supports, you could capture him."

"And what would you have me do to him once he was in my possession?"

"I'll leave it up to you."

"Would you?"

"I could offer suggestions, friendly advice," Patrick broke in. "Some best practices based on our research."

I had a feeling this was Patrick's department, and the only reason he was still allowed around this project.

"Videos have helped with Joyful Justice's recruitment," I said. "Not that I would know anything about the inner workings of that organization, of course. But I'm sure you've all seen the YouTube channel."

"Yes," Martha said. "You have experience with this type of, promotion, shall we say?"

"Promotion, yes."

The videos were not my idea. In fact, when the first ones were made, I was in a drug-induced coma. But there's that old saying, fake it till you make it. And right then I was faking a whole bunch—like that there wasn't a storm cloud shooting out lightning bolts and rolling thunder hovering above my head. I just hoped that I made it.

EK

They gave Zerzan and me rooms next door to each other, on the same hall as Bobby. My room was an interior space with skylights, but no windows out.

I slept naked between clean sheets with Blue by my feet. I dreamt that I was floating in the sky, surrounded by a powerful storm, looking down at a war-torn landscape, watching the wind, rain and lightning whip through the artillery-ravaged world, picking up bodies and tossing them here and there, destroying everything in the storm's path. I floated in the eye— surrounded by the gentle rise and fall of Blue's snores.

In the morning, I woke as the sun lit the cloudless, blue sky. I felt well-rested, well-fed, and totally insane, not sure if this world was real or the one from my dream. Were they the same?

Intercepting a convoy, killing a bunch of men, and capturing one of them sounded like a task perfect for my thunderstorm of madness. Following Bobby's lead into battle seemed like a long time coming.

It was up to Zerzan to decide what to do with Abu Mohammad al-Baghdadi once she had him. The man was the worst of the worst. He certainly deserved to be decapitated.

Would she do it, though? Not that she wasn't cold-blooded enough, but I didn't think she was that kind of leader. Zerzan's fight was about protecting her land, her people and her family. She didn't place her faith in a god who told her to chop off the heads of infidels.

So what would she do? What would she do with a man who was so evil? Torture him? Show him mercy?

There was a knock at my door. Blue jumped off the bed. I checked the peephole and saw Bobby standing there. "Gimme five," I said.

"I'll wait." He looked up and down the hall and there was a tick in his jaw. I'd never seen him look like that before, and it made the lightning above me crackle louder—something was coming.

I dressed quickly in the FGI uniform I'd worn the day before and then unlocked the door. Bobby rushed in and closed it behind him, putting the deadbolt back into place.

"We need to get out of here."

"What?"

"We need to go right now."

"That's crazy. We just made this whole deal. We're going to get Abu Mohammad al-Baghdadi."

"You can't go."

"Why not?"

Bobby stepped closer to me and leaned in. "They're going to kill you."

"Who?"

"Patrick wants you dead and Martha understands it's the safer option. I did everything I could to convince them to keep you alive. I thought I'd succeeded, but they are planning on killing you during the raid."

"I don't think Patrick or Martha can kill me."

"Of course not them personally." Bobby frowned. "The men we're taking with us. They are gonna kill you." Bobby's eyebrows were knitted together and his expression was grim, his body tense.

"I've never seen you look so concerned."

"Aren't you listening to me? I can't keep you safe. We have to leave now. Otherwise..."

"You're leading the mission. Why not just bring guys you trust?"

"You can't trust anyone. Not really, Sydney. They can pay any one of these guys enough to do it." He looked around, like maybe one of those "guys" was in the room.

"Why go through all the rigmarole? Why not just kill me here? Besides, what about me being a useful asset?"

"They needed you to get Zerzan." Bobby held up one finger. "They think they'll lose her if she knows they killed you." A second finger went up. "You were considered an asset by Homeland Security and then Mary got killed and reports got filed and you've gone from an asset of Homeland Security to a risk to the CIA." Three fingers in the air, three reasons I should die.

"But if they kill me, they still risk losing Zerzan. Obviously, she wouldn't trust them after this."

"Not obviously." Bobby hissed. "It will look like an accident. Like you died from friendly fire. Zerzan is not going to give up her cause. She's not going to give up Abu Mohammad al-Baghdadi because you get killed. She'll still need all the things she needs right now."

A loud clap of thunder rumbled over Bobby's next words. A wind lifted my hair and I felt static electricity everywhere—that strange sensation right before lightning strikes. I was done. Totally insane. Why run? To live? Wasn't I already dead? I'd done more good in the world as a dead person, a martyr, than I ever had as a living, breathing woman—maybe it was time to end this. End it all.

"I'm going."

"Great, let's go." Bobby grabbed my elbow and began to walk toward the door but I pulled back. He looked at me.

"I meant I'm going on the raid."

"What? No. Neither of us is going on the raid. Both of us are getting the fuck out of here."

"Look, this is important. This is a chance to turn this thing around. Do you get how powerful Zerzan is? Do you understand that if we can convince women to fight the way that men do, that we could change the world?"

The sizzle of lightning agreed with me, its electric voice crackling in my skull— *That girl with the gun back at the safe house, she's the future, not you. You're over.*

"You won't be around to see that change because you will be dead."

"It doesn't matter."

Bobby grabbed me by both my biceps. "Of course it matters! You matter."

"Let go of me." My voice was calm and low. Blue growled, backing me up.

Bobby stepped away, holding his hands out. "I can't believe you. A fucking martyr."

"I know. Isn't it crazy?" I smiled as a lightning bolt brushed my cheek. "I never thought I was the martyr type."

"I'm not just going to let you get killed. There's no way, Sydney. You might care more about saving the world than yourself, but I care more about you."

"That's kind of sweet but also kind of totally selfish and dickish."

Bobby's jaw dropped. "Dickish? Selfish? I'm trying to save your life."

"Yeah, so you can have me around. Once I'm out of the way, Martha and Patrick will still support Zerzan, right? They want this project to work."

"Yes, they do."

"You better get back to your room. We have a raid to prepare for."

"I won't change your mind?"

"Sorry, but no."

Bobby started for the door, with his hand on the knob he turned back to me. "You know I have your back."

"I know." He held my gaze, his eyes both hard and soft—an impossible combination—we are all a host of contradictions. Like lightning indoors, rainfall without wetness, thunder without sound. Bobby was evil and good, selfish and selfless, loathsome and loving, all things and all people. We are all one—every thing on the planet is made from the same vibrating atoms—the only thing separating us is consciousness. And mine was no longer functioning.

"Be brave," Bobby said. It was the first time I'd heard Robert Maxim use Joyful Justice's catchphrase. I smiled, more touched by it than I would've expected.

"Be brave," I responded.

Bobby left and I turned to Blue. He was standing by my side looking up at me. Somehow, I thought he knew what the conversation was about. When I offered up my own life, in a way I was freeing him. Blue might die trying to protect me, but I hoped that he would survive and find a more peaceful life.

I put my hand on the crown of his head. Then squatted down so that we were face-to-face. "I love you." Blue stepped forward, pushing his brow into my shoulder.

I wrapped my arms around him, pressed my face into his neck and breathed in his musky scent. He still smelled like pine and the sweet rot of the forest floor despite the bath I'd given him the night before.

We stayed like that for an indeterminable amount of time. It felt so safe and so comforting to hold him and breathe him in. Dogs offer us something that no other animal can. Blue's loyalty and love was unquestioning and mine to him was the same.

It was impossible to share this kind of bond with a human—at least for me. There was no team in the world as powerful as Blue and me. We'd found each other in this giant, crazy, unjust world, and that fact gave me faith.

When I stepped into that pound in Bushwick, Brooklyn almost five years ago, I was looking for something in my life worth holding onto. Blue had been skinny and skittish and gigantic. The man working at the shelter tried to convince me to go with something smaller, more appropriate for a young woman living in a small apartment in a big city.

But the moment I saw his mismatched eyes and the way he hardly fit in the cage, I knew that Blue was meant for me. He cost me a hundred and eight dollars. That included the cost of neutering him, which I was supposed to return and have done once he put on some weight, but I never went back.

When I brought Blue home that day, I had no idea how important he would become. I thought I was just getting a pet, but that's not what happens when you adopt a dog. Even if he had never saved my life, even if he hadn't been with me through so much, he still would've changed my life because that's what dogs do. They fill a hole in you. They soak up pain and loneliness. They are at once a sponge and a calming salve.

As I hugged him under the skylight in that room in the middle of a war zone, and I breathed in his scent, Blue comforted me in a way that only a dog can. He was more than a partner, more than a protector, even more than a best friend. Blue was my dog. And there is nothing in this world as great as a dog.

CHAPTER SEVENTEEN

Abu Mohammad al-Baghdadi's convoy was expected to pass through a narrow valley at around 1 a.m. By 7 p.m., we were in position. The equipment and weapons were brand new, of the highest quality, and without a doubt the right stuff for the job.

There were a total of eleven of us. Bobby, Zerzan, myself, and Blue, plus another seven men. All were former FGI employees and now contractors for our new company, Dog Fight Investigations.

I'd met them at breakfast. Well, I'd already met two of them when they'd picked me up in the helicopter. All the men were similar in build and skill sets. As we shared plates full of eggs and toast, I took time to look each man in the eye. To try to guess which one was planning to kill me.

Philip Gray: short, blond hair. Well they all had short hair, didn't they? A button nose and cheerful, green eyes. His lips were plump and feminine, his teeth charmingly crooked. He looked to be about thirty-five years old. Just enough wrinkles to make him truly handsome but not quite enough to make him look old. Philip had broad shoulders and wore a tight, black T-shirt with the FGI emblem on the breast, tucked into his cargo pants. He ate quickly, shoveling the food into his mouth, holding the handle of his fork in a fist. He didn't do a lot of talking. Mostly he just laughed at the other men.

Terry McGillicuddy: He'd picked me up in the helicopter and was the one making everybody laugh. He was the shortest of all of them, which wasn't short—just shy of six feet. His hair was dark and trimmed tight to his skull. His eyes were brown and sparkling with laughter for most of the breakfast. Terry wore the same black T-shirt with the FGI symbol. His biceps bulged and the tight muscles of his shoulders cut through the thin material. He ate more eggs than anybody else but avoided the carbs, at one point making a joke about the glycemic index. You had to be there.

Avery Lindenhurst: He sat next to Terry and the men appeared to be close. He'd been the other man on the helicopter that had picked me up. Avery was the biggest guy in the group and had the longest hair, which wasn't saying much. But his golden curls had started to grow over his ears. He had hazel eyes, a long strong nose, and a cleft chin. He didn't laugh out loud, but his large shoulders shook as Terry cracked him up. His FGI black T-shirt looked like it hardly fit, too tight on such a big man. It was also more faded than the others, the black having been through too many washes. Did it have some kind of sentimental value? Or, along with the extra length of his hair, was it just a matter of being low maintenance?

James Gavioli: Italian American with jet-black hair, big, brown eyes, and olive skin; he reminded me of people I'd grown up with. He was from Yonkers—and sounded like it. He volleyed back and forth verbally with Terry, setting him up so that Terry could make the slam-dunks. I had a friend in high school who came from a big, Italian family, Jill Luciano. And James' banter reminded me of dinners at her house.

In addition to that blast from the past, he also shared my brother's name. If James tried to kill me, it would be hard. I didn't want to fight him. He reminded me too much of a part of my life that I liked, in hindsight. Though at the time, if you'd told me those high school years, when my brother was still alive and I was getting invited over to Jill's house for dinner, would be the best of my life, I would have laughed. I would have pointed to my alcoholic mother and my dilapidated house and told you I was getting out of there as fast as possible. Of course now, I'd give anything to go back to that time. To see my brother James one more time. To spend just one moment outside the prison cell of my failing mind.

Taylor Maudlin: A California surfer dude with very blond hair, deeply tanned skin, sparkling, light blue eyes, and a disarming grin. He wasn't as bulky as the other guys. His laugh was full and friendly. A former Navy SEAL, like most of the guys, Taylor told mc how much he missed thc ocean, twice. Once in context and once just out of the blue. Was he telling me because he felt guilty about taking money in order to kill me and return to the sea he missed?

Connor Oberon: the first thing I noticed was the scar on his face. It looked like a blade had sliced him from his left eyebrow across the bridge of his nose and on to his right cheek. His head was shaved completely. His eyes were incredibly dark, almost entirely black. There was only a slight variation between the pupil and iris. Connor hardly laughed, hardly spoke. He ate his food with a slow and steady determination. Chewing each bite a uniform number of times—I counted, and it was twenty-three. Then swallow, followed by a sip of milk, a deep breath in through his nose, out his mouth, and then another bite of food. Those dark eyes scanned the room. His large shoulders hunched forward as if he were a dog protecting his bowl.

Of course, he seemed like the most obvious risk. Dark and scary, clearly with a violent past. But I didn't fear him. There was something noble about him. I didn't think a man who ate like that was interested in throwing away his honor in exchange for cash. But it wasn't just my own instincts that made me trust him: Blue had wagged his tail at Connor.

Deacon Tanner: a Texan, the oldest of the men. He filled out his crisp, new FGI shirt in a way that made Zerzan keep glancing at him. Dimples and a Texas drawl added to his charm. He was quiet but made a few comments here and there. Keeping things light, doing his part to help Terry keep the breakfast conversation going. He was looking at Zerzan as much as she was looking at him. Every time he caught her eye, he gave her a dimple-filled smile and she'd force a scowl.

I didn't have a chance to speak to Zerzan before the meal began, so when Bobby stood up, signaling the end, I moved around the table toward her. Deacon had picked up Zerzan's tray and offered to bus it for her, flashing his dimples one more time. She frowned. "I can do it."

"Of course you can," Deacon said with another grin. "But it would be my pleasure."

Before Zerzan could respond, she spotted me, and I raised my eyebrows and tilted my head toward the ladies' room. She gave Deacon one more frown before joining me.

I checked that all the stalls were empty. Zerzan watched me, her arms crossed and the frown still on her face.

"Someone is going to try to kill me today."

"Yes..." She raised her eyebrows as in, *duh*.

"I mean, someone on our team."

Zerzan's frown deepened. "Why?"

"It's better if I'm not around. I'm a liability to this whole operation. They needed me to broker the deal with you because you trust me. And they need me to die in a way that looks like it's legitimate so that you will continue to trust them."

"How do you know this?"

"Bobby told me."

"And you can trust him?"

"I can."

"Who will try?"

"I don't know, one of the guys we just met. I'm just telling you this so that if I do die today, you'll know what happened. But I think that—"

Zerzan interrupted me. "You're not going to die."

"Hey," I held up a hand. "I appreciate your faith. But, it's always good to be prepared for the worst." She started to respond, but I pushed on. "Promise me that you will continue to work with Bobby to get what you need."

"Agreed."

I smiled. "Well, that was easier than I thought."

Zerzan shrugged. "I know how important what I'm doing is. I also know you're not going to die today."

Only half of me hoped she was right. The other half—the one that had noticed the fissure of lightning that circled the ceiling of the bathroom, shooting out sparks of madness—was ready to end this. One last gasp, one last attempt to do something good. To exact some kind of justice in this sick world. Then peace. Rest. An ending.

EK

Philip (the one with the pretty mouth), Taylor (the surfer dude), James (the Italian), and Connor (the scary one) were our snipers. The road below was paved, a ribbon of black through a sea of gray sand. Zerzan, Blue, and I would be pulling the target from his vehicle and moving him onto the helicopter. Deacon (the Texan) was our pilot and Terry (the joker) and Avery (the joker's best bud), would assist us in the transport.

According to our intelligence—well, according to Martha's intelligence—our target would be traveling in a convoy of six vehicles. Six Toyota trucks with mounted machine guns and a Land Cruiser. And our target would be in the Land Cruiser.

Three fighters per truck, two in the cab, one in the back. Another three men in the Land Cruiser guarding our target. A total of twenty-two men.

We planned on ambushing the convoy at a place where the road barely fit between opposing faces of the mountains. The cliffs rose up starkly on either side; only small trees and spindly bushes clung to the rocky surface.

The section of road between the cliffs was long enough that you could trap a convoy of seven vehicles.

Night descended while we waited. Zerzan, Blue, and I sat on a rocky ledge thirty feet above the ground. There was a path to the road which could be traversed quickly, but needed concentration.

Zerzan and I were dressed in black with helmets and flak jackets. We even had night vision goggles if we needed them. But I doubted we would, considering that the convoy's headlights would likely make it too bright for the goggles.

Our four snipers—Taylor, James, Connor, and Philip—were in position above us. They were collectively responsible for taking out the eighteen men in the Toyota trucks. The snipers would first take out the lead and follow vehicles, locking the Land Cruiser in the center of the narrow cut between the cliffs. The SUV may or may not be bulletproof.

Luckily for us, our target was burned as a child, so half his face looked like melted cheese, making him easy to identify.

Once the lead and follow vehicles were disabled, the snipers would kill the rest of our target's protection in the ensuing gun battle, at which point Zerzan and I were charged with extracting our man alive from the Land Cruiser. With help from Terry and Avery, we'd load him onto the helicopter and away we'd fly.

The helicopter waited on a plateau at the top of the mountain. It was our evac point if anything went wrong. I glanced up the mountainside; it was almost sheer, with just enough rock outcroppings to make it climbable.

My mind was clear and yet fingers of lightning radiated around me, along with the low thrum of thunder vibrating in my ears.

Rather than a distraction, these figments of my broken mind helped to center my focus.

Our mission was to capture Abu Mohammad al-Baghdadi and use him to begin a women-led revolution that would take down Daesh.

Yet, to think in terms that broad was not helpful in a battle situation. My only goal could be to do my best and keep Blue and myself alive for as long as possible.

Clearly, I was broken. The years of anger and violence, the many injuries both physical and psychological, had destroyed me.

This could be my final act.

That brought me a sense of calm that I hadn't felt in half a decade. Perhaps I'd never felt it before. I'd always wondered about my purpose and questioned my life. But now, as I sat on the edge of the rock formation, my feet dangling into empty space, it was obvious what was important. And it wasn't me.

For years I'd been saying that I didn't matter, that I didn't care.

But I acted as if I was the only thing that mattered; my own thirst for blood and revenge guided my every move.

Now was my chance to finish it. With this one sacrifice, this one final chance at salvation, I could help start the revolution and leave this world, hopefully, a better place.

Blue touched his nose to my elbow and I laid a hand on the top of his head. He sat next to me, our bodies close together.

I imagined him disappearing into this wilderness, finding a pack of wolves to live with. Finally free of the burden of me.

"I see them," Phillip's voice said in my ear.

They were early. We had not expected them until all signs of the sun had gone, and the moon's dominion was established.

"They have motorcyclists with them. An additional seven, no, ten men."

The numbers didn't matter. Zerzan was an unstoppable force and her destiny was already written. She was going to change the world. It didn't matter how many men tried to stop her; she'd send them all to Hell.

The rumble of pistons pumping reached us. It sounded like the final complaints of a dying society.

Adrenaline pumped into my system. The snipers checked in over the line. Everyone was ready. Everything was in place. The action was about to begin.

CHAPTER EIGHTEEN

The first truck came into view, followed quickly by the second and third. They were blasting through this narrow passage, understanding that it was the most dangerous part of their journey.

The gunfire that popped the front tires of the lead vehicle was almost silent. The speeding truck swerved out of control, leaving the paved road and smashing into the rock face, crumpling the front end. Smoke spewed from under the hood. The guard who'd been in the bed, manning the mounted machine gun, flew over his weapon and smashed onto the rocks before landing on the steaming hood, denting it further.

The second vehicle careened into the back end of the first, becoming wedged between the turned truck and the rock face. The third truck stopped in time to avoid a collision. Yelling started as bullets flew.

From our vantage point, we saw a sniper round execute the soldier manning the machine gun in the back of the third vehicle. Then another round took out the gunman in the second.

The men on motorcycles pulled up and jumped off their bikes. One went down, his brain exploding onto the road. They were trying to push the trucks out of the way to create an opening for the Land Cruiser to escape.

The back of the convoy was not visible to us until we began to climb down the mountain. Still hidden within the folds of the rocks, we saw that the follow vehicle was also under fire and its occupants were being killed quickly and efficiently.

The Land Cruiser sat in the middle of the melee, tinted glass windows and bright white headlights, a center of calm in a sea of calamity.

Stars began to pop out in the darkening sky, as if the sound of the gunfire had awakened them. The shadowy space between the high cliff faces was darker than the flat plains on either side. I could see the last vestiges of light down the road, but darkness now reigned where our battle waged.

A Daesh fighter behind one of the still-functioning mounted guns fired wildly into the mountain. Rock exploded off the cliff face; sharp shards of ancient soil flew through the air, raining down on the blacktop.

A sniper's bullet knocked the man off the gun; he fell over the side of the truck, his limbs spiraling, and landed on the pavement, dead.

Zerzan and I stayed hidden, crouching in the shadows at the base of the cliff side, a small, scrubby tree hiding us from the men who ran back and forth, trying to survive.

No compassion, no sadness. I felt nothing. Lightning flashed and thunder rolled. The stiff wind of my madness carried away all fear as I stepped out from our shelter. Blue touched his nose to my hip.

Zerzan moved with me.

No one noticed us.

Three men were pushing the front vehicles blocking the road—they had gotten one to the side and were working on the second. A sniper bullet took one of the men out. He fell against the truck, his blood spattering a brilliant red coating on the dusty surface.

The other two men didn't look at their fallen comrade; their purpose was as clear as my own.

The second truck budged; they yelled in triumph. Another bullet struck one of them, piercing his thigh, blood and muscle exploding out of the exit wound. The man stumbled but with a feral scream, kept pushing.

The truck cleared, the last dying light of day so close, the open road calling.

The Land Cruiser roared to life. It slammed through the narrow opening, spinning one of the trucks to the side.

Sniper rounds tinged against the bumper and back windows, but did not breach the SUV.

"Stay, Blue." I pointed back to our hiding place and he returned to the black shadows.

The thump of the helicopter broke through the rumble of thunder.

Zerzan and I crossed to one of the fallen bikes, stained with its rider's blood, his body still slumped next to it. I picked it up, climbed on, and Zerzan got on the back.

A soldier noticed us then, his eyes widening so that I could see the whites in the dark shadows of the steep valley. Zerzan fired behind me and his head rocked back, taking his body down with it.

I revved the engine, feeling the power between my thighs.

We shot forward, Zerzan wrapping one arm around my waist, the other holding her pistol. One of the men who'd helped to push the lead truck out of the way reached out, a crazed and desperate attempt to stop us. His hand touched my elbow, I felt his fingers, the warmth of his skin through my sleeve, for only a moment before Zerzan knocked him away, her gun connecting with his wrist with a sickening crack as the bone gave out.

Then we were out in the open, the sky giant above us, midnight blue, rich, and darkening fast. Stars burned, light a billion years old sparkling like it was brand new.

The moon, a silver sliver at the horizon, followed our progress as we raced to catch up with the Land Cruiser which was barely visible through the thick cloud of dust rising up behind it.

The helicopter flew over, beating air down upon us, thwapping loudly, faster than us. It maneuvered in front of the land cruiser and turned back to it, firing into the front end.

A tire caught fire, exploded off, and rolled, flaming down the road. I swerved to avoid it. Through my side mirror, I saw it continue on its own path, the stench of burning rubber filling my nose.

The Land Cruiser slowed, sparks flying from its destroyed tires as it continued to roll on its rims. The flashes turned to lightning in my vision, spidering out into the distance, spreading across the horizon, filling the night with bright, white light.

The Land Cruiser came to a stop. I slowed down, the engine of the bike chortling. The Land Cruiser's windows and doors remained closed, the black tint hiding the occupants, the bulletproof glass protecting them from us.

I rolled around to the front. The headlights lit up the night, illuminating white smoke that rolled off the rims. The helicopter hovered right above the ground, dust and smoke billowing around it.

Zerzan jumped off the bike and in two long strides hopped up onto the hood of the Land Cruiser. Both hands gripping her weapon, she fired into the windshield, spacing her bullets evenly, starting with the passenger side and moving toward the driver's.

The bullets ricocheted off the glass, flying back at her, landing with small tinging sounds on the black top. The crack of the windshield came on her tenth shot.

She shot again and again. Then raised her leg and kicked hard, breaking through into the vehicle.

The yelling of deep, male voices sounded from inside the SUV.

I dropped the bike and pulled my pistol. Zerzan shot the driver and then dove into the vehicle. More gunshots lit up the interior. Black silhouettes were caught in the flashing lights; arms up, weapons raised, bodies going slack, heads kicking back.

The back door flew open. A dead body fell out, the eyes wide, staring up at the sky above.

Another man fell out, landing on his hands and knees, this one alive. Zerzan came out after him. A graze on her cheek pumped blood, spilling it down her neck, soaking her shirt.

The man on the ground looked up at me. His face was twisted with scar tissue. I grabbed him and started hauling him toward the helicopter.

Zerzan helped, taking his other arm. His head swiveled between the two of us.

Avery and Terry ran up to us and took the man, throwing him through the open helicopter door. Zerzan jumped in after him.

"I have to get Blue!" I yelled. Zerzan nodded, turned to the captive, and pulled her knife, a smile crawling across her blood-soaked face.

I returned to the bike, picked it up, climbed on, and kicked it to life. Leaning over the handlebars, I raced back toward the shadows.

"Rye." Bobby's voice, calm and relaxed in my ear. "Meet at the top of the mountain. We will evac together." The valley loomed ahead, the headlamps of the disabled vehicles lighting it up like a stage. "There are no combatants left. You should have a clear route to us."

I slowed down as I entered the battle zone, maneuvering around fallen bodies and abandoned trucks. The sky was full black now, the headlights columns of white light, illuminating the destruction. Bodies everywhere, splayed on the road, slumped over in the cabs, hanging off the truck beds. The coppery scent of blood and acrid smoke of ammunition fire cloyed at me.

Blue stepped out of the shadows.

I stopped the bike and turned it off before dropping it to the pavement.

We were the only two things alive in that cramped space between the cliffs. All the animals had fled at the sharp crack of gunfire and deep throttle of engines. Blood dripped, thunder pealed, and lightning flashed all around me.

"Let's go," I said, tapping my thigh. Blue fell in next to me and I began to climb.

"We've got incoming," Philip's voice in my ear. "Another convoy. I'm guessing it's their backup." Sweat trickled under my helmet, so I ripped it off, letting it fall down the mountain, bouncing against rocks, and spiraling over ledges toward the ground.

"They've got a tank."

Blue jumped up ahead of me, spraying small rocks down onto my face and arms. I spit, clearing dust off my lips.

"Sydney, hurry up," Bobby said.

"I'm going as fast as I can." But I still had a long way to go. I craned my neck, peering up the mountainside. Lightning snaked across my vision.

The loud boom of a weapon was followed by the cracking of rock. Deacon's Texas drawl, "We have to go now."

"Rye, we'll be back for you."

The thwap of the helicopter receded as I continued to climb.

EK

My hand crested the rock, gripping the dusty surface of the plateau and I pulled myself up. Blue was behind me, waiting for me to get fully onto the ledge before following. A bullet sank into my shoulder, sending a sharp pain sizzling through my body, and releasing adrenaline into my veins.

My heart pumped, spreading the hormone quickly as I rolled back off the cliff, landing with a thud onto the rock below. Blue jumped out of my way, scrambling onto another rock ledge and disappearing into the low brush.

I pulled my pistol and aimed it at the sky, waiting for someone to pop their head over the edge, to finish me off.

Clouds, city sidewalk gray, drifted lazily above.

My heartbeat thundered in my ears. My breath came sharp and painful, each inhalation pushing the wound against my clothing, every exhalation, pulling it free. I bit my lip to keep from making any sound.

Time passed. Were they coming for me?

Or would I have to go to them?

Where was Blue?

I rolled onto my good side, getting my feet under me and stood. My shot arm, the left one, hung useless by my side.

I followed the path Blue had taken into the brush. I didn't see him, but the path his big body had taken was clear. I followed it, finding a gentler path that led to the plateau.

I stayed low, my pistol in my hand, sweat slicking my palm, plastering my hair to my head, dripping down my neck.

A bullet sliced through the vegetation and slammed into my calf, bringing me to my knees.

A black clad figure stood to my left, his rifle raised, aiming at my head. I aimed my pistol, but Blue got him first, rocketing out of the brush, biting into the man's forearm, and taking him down to the ground.

Stumbling forward on my good leg, I ran at the two of them. The figure in black pulled a knife; it caught the starlight, glinting at me, sending a thick line of lightning shooting out of it, connecting with the pain in my leg and burning there.

I threw myself on him, grabbing for the knife, keeping it from stabbing into Blue.

The figure on the ground wore the same style of helmet I'd tossed off, his night vision goggles lowered over his eyes, but I recognized his lips. Those pretty pink lips of Philip.

It didn't matter, though, which man came to kill me. He was just the weapon of the powerful people who wanted me dead. He didn't matter. I didn't matter. Nothing that happened there, under this starry sky on the top of that mountain, could stop what we'd set in motion tonight.

That didn't mean I was gonna let this motherfucker stab my dog though.

Philip struck out, elbowing me hard in the side of the head. I fell off, taking the knife with me, my vision clouding, growing dark at the edges.

Blue growled, his mouth full of Philip's flesh. Philip hit me again, this time with the butt of his pistol, swinging it through the air, connecting with my temple.

I rolled away, the knife in my fist. Thunder vibrated every pore. Lighting blinded me. But I felt no pain, and, when I came to my feet, I used my good leg to launch myself back at Philip. I stabbed his own knife into his neck. His lips moved, blood welling out of his throat, bubbling up to his mouth.

I knocked off his goggles, wanting to see his eyes. All I saw was electricity filling the sockets, nothing but light glowing out of his skull.

I stumbled back, falling into the dirt, my breath coming hard and fast, rasping through me, storm wind rattling naked branches.

Blue licked my face. My vision darkened. I lay back. Blue whined. "It's over, boy. You're free."

He barked. My eyes shut. Blue howled, pulling me back, my eyes fluttered open at the mournful sound. He was staring down at me. He barked again and looked to his left. I followed his gaze.

A white dog stood there. Almost as big as Blue. I blinked. Moonlight made its coat sparkle like snow on a sunny day.

A figure shrouded in a black burka appeared next to it. They approached slowly. I heard the tingling of bells.

The woman stood over me, the long, black burka rising up. I followed the folds until I reached her eyes. They were shining with starlight. "Are you real?" I rasped.

She nodded.

The blackness of her burka grew, filling my vision, blacking out the world, enveloping me in its darkness.

Peace. At last.

EK

Turn the page to read an excerpt from
In Sheep's Clothing, Sydney Rye Mysteries Book 9, or purchase it now and continue reading Sydney's next adventure:
emilykimelman.com/ISC

EK

SNEAK PEEK
IN SHEEP'S CLOTHING, SYDNEY RYE MYSTERIES BOOK 9

Animals had gotten to the corpse, tearing the flesh off the skeleton and exposing the bone. The man standing over the body, his green-blue gaze the same shade as Caribbean waters if they ever froze, stared into the empty eye sockets of his former employee. Bloody, torn flesh, ribboned by some bird, hung down the dead man's cheeks.

Softness is the first thing eaten.

A breeze stirred the pine trees, their needles tapping against each other, whispering in a private conversation. Robert Maxim scanned the ground again, his gaze tracing the fight.

Blood was splattered in the dirt. A lot of it. Phillip had died slowly. He'd tried to pull the knife free, but the black, blood crusted handle still protruded from the dead man's throat. Philip's left forearm appeared particularly ravaged, probably from Sydney Rye's dog, Blue.

The sharpshooter's weapons were gone, unless you counted that knife in his neck.

Next to Philip, a depression in the dirt—the outline of a medium-sized woman punctuated with pools of blood—kept pulling Robert's attention.

Sydney Rye plunged the knife home and then fell over, succumbing to her own wounds. Which, judging by the amount of blood on the ground, were grave.

Robert turned slowly, observing every rock, stick, scuff and depression in the dirt.

Deep scratches marked where Blue leapt, his nails digging into the dirt as his back legs propelled him into the air. There were other dog prints, too. Not as large as Blue's, but far bigger than the common dogs found in this area, the contested territory along the Syrian-Iraqi border.

A tuft of white fur fluttered on a low branch. Bobby approached it slowly, carefully placing his booted feet where no clues lay. The fur was softer than Sydney's mutt's rough, wolf-like coat. Bobby pulled the white fluff off the branch and slipped it into his pocket.

Footsteps approached, soft thuds cushioned by pine needles. "Stay back." The intensity of Robert's emotions roughened his voice into a dangerous growl.

"That's our man there. Gotta pack him up, get him out of here. Animals are already getting to him," Conner said. Another sharpshooter who'd worked with Philip for years, Conner's bald head and scarred face made him look dangerous. *And he was.* Had Conner known that Philip took money to try to kill Sydney Rye?

"I need more time."

Conner disappeared, silent and patient.

Robert crouched down and looked at the dirt. *Goats.* Goats had come through here after the fight.

Sydney Rye didn't get up and walk away. Someone carried her, and they managed not to leave a trail of blood. The bald tread of a homemade boot wound through the forest, the goat hooves obscuring all but the smallest trace.

Either a small man or tall woman, traveling with a dog and a herd of goats, had carried Sydney Rye away. *Why?*

Herders passed through here on their way from one village to another. The person must be under Daesh protection...or desperate. Why take a bleeding woman? That injured, she'd be useless, the amount of work to patch her up hardly worth the price.

Unless, of course, this herder knew who Sydney Rye was.

Robert Maxim would pay any price to get her back. But few people knew that, let alone a random goat herder.

Conner appeared again, his silent figure a reminder that time was tight and the location not fully secured. "You can take him away." Robert did not look up. Conner disappeared back into the trees, going to get the stretcher and other men to help carry Philip.

Robert didn't think of Philip as a traitor. What was he committing treason against? A corporation? His personal relationship with Robert Maxim? His loyalty to the other men on his team?

None of that really mattered. Working for a defense company like Fortress Global International or Dog Fight Investigations wasn't the same as being a member of the United States Armed Forces.

Robert never served his nation, but the rest of his team were all veterans. Like Robert, these men now fought not for honor and glory, but for money. Philip had accepted money to try to kill a member of his team. Albeit, a recent member.

This was the first time Philip had even met Sydney Rye. He didn't know anything about her. Didn't have to, in order to try to kill her. However, knowing she was almost impossible to kill would've kept him alive.

Philip widowed his wife and left his kid without a father.

Robert shook his head at the man's stupidity before taking one more look at the scene— Phillip's prone body, the spattering of blood, the marks in the dirt outlining the fight—before turning and leaving.

He walked through the trees, ducking under low branches and pushing others aside. The rich scent of sap in his nose blotted out the metallic tang of blood.

It wasn't normal for Robert Maxim to feel emotions. He'd spent a lifetime controlling and containing them—only allowing what was useful to surface to his consciousness. But as he walked through those trees, his feet sinking into the soft earth, his heart clenched with fear.

Fear was the worst of all the emotions. The one that Robert Maxim had done the best at conquering. But that was the problem with Rye, wasn't it? She made him *feel* things; she made him do things—she controlled him without even trying.

Robert reached the helicopter and climbed in next to the pilot. Deacon, originally from Texas, had an easy smile and covert ops military experience. His gaze drifted over to Robert, but he didn't say anything.

Did his men know?

Robert checked his face, making sure it was arranged into a hard, cold mask of indifference and calculation.

The men returned with Philip's body and loaded it into the back of the helicopter. Robert gave the word, and the bird lifted off. They rose up above the trees and tilted to the north, passing over the narrow road still littered with bodies and broken vehicles.

Whoever took Sydney didn't have much of a head start. Robert directed Deacon to do a quick scan of the area. They flew low and fast over the trees in the direction of the goat's hoof prints. The elevation dropped off steeply, the mountain craggy and rife with caves, bare of anything but the hardiest vegetation.

The thwap of the helicopter blades and the static of the radio coming through Robert's headphones couldn't cover up the rapid beat of his heart in his ears. Robert's eyes raked over the desolate landscape, looking for any kind of movement on the ground. A herd of goats, two dogs, a badly injured woman and another person couldn't have gotten far...*but there were so many places to hide.*

After thirty minutes, Robert nodded his head, a small gesture to indicate that they should head back to the base. The chopper left the mountains and flew over the desert plains, a wide and empty space devoid of human activity.

They returned to the army base in Turkish territory and Robert headed toward the low-slung building with its tinted reflective doors that housed the offices and barracks. It looked like a hundred other bases he'd visited. *But this was different.*

Robert Maxim was having *feelings*. He tried to wrestle them under control and smooth them away as he opened the door.

Martha's assistant picked up the phone to announce him. Robert strode to the door and opened it, not waiting for permission.

The CIA director sat behind her desk, hands folded on her stomach. In her late fifties, Martha Emerson had a helmet of blonde hair streaked with silver and green eyes the color of golf course grass, and just as flat.

"You brought back the bodies?"

The skin around Robert's eyes tightened. *She said bodies, plural.*

"Just one body."

Martha raised her eyebrows, recognizing her mistake. *She hadn't expected Philip to survive his assault on Sydney, but figured he'd manage to kill her nonetheless.*

Everyone underestimated Sydney Rye.

"What happened?" Martha pushed on, not verbalizing the tension in the room—they both knew she'd ordered the hit. But that was the way of this world, of Robert's world. Never admit what's really happening; always play the game.

Except Sydney never did.

Her face filled his mind's eye: mercury gray eyes, black hair with thick bangs tickling at her lashes, those scars around her left eye, faded but still tightening the skin, still a reminder of her fierceness—if her hard gaze, taut lips, harsh words and tight body weren't enough. As if anyone who saw her could doubt for a moment that she would kill them...or save them, depending on her point of view.

"It seems that Philip and Sydney had a fight. Philip died."

Martha frowned. "And your girl? Is she okay?"

Robert let a twitch of a smile curl his lip before answering. "She's not my girl."

"She's your business partner?"

"As a woman in a man's world, I'd think you'd be more sensitive to sexist stereotypes. Referring to her as my girl, diminishes her, doesn't it?"

Martha cocked her head, her eyes lighting—she'd caught a tone in his voice, a clue. "She's alive?

"I don't know." Emotion gurgled in his chest, and his mind fought to banish it, keep it out of his gaze, where it could do irreparable harm.

He couldn't keep Sydney Rye out of his mind.

Lord knows, he tried.

"What do you mean?" An edge of annoyance sharpened Martha's

tone, as if being cagey was offensive to her. What a joke coming from a director at the CIA.

"She's gone. Philip's body was there, lots of blood, clearly a scuffle." He made it all sound so casual. "But she's missing. Possibly captured."

"That's not good." The lines around Martha's mouth deepened. "She could be used as leverage with Zerzan. Do you think they will try to make a trade for Abu Mohammad al-Baghdadi?"

"I don't know."

Taking Abu Mohammad al-Baghdadi prisoner was important for the CIA's plan to destabilize the Islamic State's caliphate—and selling weapons to Zerzan and her Kurdish fighting group was key in Robert's plan to get even richer. But Robert only *cared* about getting Sydney back.

Daesh soldiers believed in the divine providence of their state and Abu Mohammad al-Baghdadi was one of the strongest voices, the most sanguine arguers, on behalf of the caliphate, the nation prophesied—and some believed mandated—in the Quran.

Known for his violent videos, his stark philosophical arguments, and scarred face, Abu Mohammad's capture by Zerzan was a powerful blow to the Daesh leadership. While the American government officially had nothing to do with the Peshmerga fighting force that seized him, Martha had provided the intel that left Abu Mohammad al-Baghdadi in Zerzan's grip.

"*She* got away, at least." Martha referred to Zerzan's escape. Robert had left Sydney behind to get her and Abu Mohammad al-Baghdadi out. He had then dropped Zerzan and her captive off in Kurdish territory, where her troops met her with a convoy of trucks and a tank...recently provided by Robert's new company, Dog Fight Investigations, and paid for by the US government—funds Congress approved but never saw line items for.

Those multimillions helped to ease the suffering in Robert. *At least he had money. Money. Money.*

"I don't think that Zerzan would risk her cause for a single life." Robert shrugged.

Martha held his gaze, and her pupils dilated. *She knew.* She knew how much he cared. Robert refused to look away, forcing coldness into his gaze, extinguishing the fire scalding his inside with pure icy will.

Expose nothing.

His whole life he'd practiced his poker face. *It couldn't fail him now.*

At sixteen he'd left his parents' house and became a professional gambler. With a fake ID and an unparalleled ability to count cards, he made enough money to set himself up in business. *The cocaine business.*

In Miami, in that era, cocaine ruled. And Robert Maxim set his sights on the top of the pyramid. At twenty-one, he believed that he had one of the best poker faces in the world—until he went down to Columbia to try to negotiate taking over from his distributor.

Instead, he found himself a prisoner.

Spending a year in a cage in the Colombian jungle, a ransom for the FARC, reinforced the vital lesson to hide everything except what Robert wanted his opponent to see.

He needed to leave before he gave anything else away to Martha.

Robert stood and turned to go, but Martha stopped him with a question. "We're still good? It's not as if we *needed* Sydney for this, right?"

"We're fine." Robert looked back at her—the truth of his statement in his gaze. Of course, he didn't *need* Sydney to run this business, to make this fortune, to do these deals.

He needed her to be happy. To be able to sleep. To feel like life was worth living.

To quench this goddamn fire roasting his insides.

Martha could see none of that in his gaze now, though. He shoved it right down there to his toes. The scent of the Colombian mud in his nose, the wailing of the insects at night in his ears, reminded his body and brain of the dangers that loose emotions wrought. His breath came in even, deep drafts. His fingers relaxed, shoulder blades on his back, abs tight and supportive.

Martha nodded and broke the eye contact first.

Robert kept his hands loose, his stride steady, as he traversed the airfield, headed back toward his quarters. He needed a shower; the mission had left him sweaty and dusty.

Outside his windows, the distant mountains were black spears against a sky sparkling with stars, and the air-conditioning hummed its electronic tune. He turned on the TV and went into the bathroom. The shower running, its thrumming rhythm blocking any listening devices in his space, Robert climbed in under the spray. He slid down the wall, crouching in the corner and rested his face into his hands.

Hands that had killed, caressed, grabbed, but always played to win.

He gave himself ten minutes in that white noise, under that hot spray, before turning off the shower and returning to his room. Pulling the secure phone from his safe, Robert began to dial.

He'd find Sydney Rye, but he couldn't do it alone.

EK

Continue reading *In Sheep's Clothing*: emilykimelman.com/ISC

EK

Sign up for my newsletter and stay up to date on new releases, free books, and giveaways:
emilykimelman.com/News

Join my Facebook group, *Emily Kimelman's Insatiable Readers,* **to stay up to date on sales and releases, have exclusive giveaways, and hang out with your fellow book addicts:** emilykimelman.com/EKIR.

AUTHOR'S NOTE

Thank you for reading *The Girl with the Gun*. I'm excited that you made it to my "note". I'm guessing that means that you enjoyed my story. If so, would you please write a review for *The Girl with the Gun*? You have no idea how much it warms my heart to get a new review. And this isn't just for me, mind you. Think of all the people out there who need reviews to make decisions. The children who need to be told this book is not for them. And the people about to go away on vacation who could have so much fun reading this on the plane. Consider it an act of kindness to me, to the children, to humanity.

Let people know what you thought about *The Girl with the Gun* on your favorite ebook retailer.

Thank you,

Emily

ABOUT THE AUTHOR

I write because I love to read...but I have specific tastes. I love to spend time in fictional worlds where justice is exacted with a vengeance. Give me raw stories with a protagonist who feels like a friend, heroic pets, plots that come together with a BANG, and long series so the adventure can continue. If you got this far in my book then I'm assuming you feel the same...

Sign up for my newsletter and
never miss a new release or sale:
emilykimelman.com/News

Join my Facebook group, *Emily Kimelman's Insatiable Readers,* to stay up to date on sales and releases, have exclusive giveaways, and hang out with your fellow book addicts: emilykimelman.com/EKIR.

If you've read my work and want to get in touch please do! I loves hearing from readers.
www.emilykimelman.com
emily@emilykimelman.com

facebook.com/EmilyKimelman
instagram.com/emilykimelman

EMILY'S BOOKSHELF

Visit www.emilykimelman.com to purchase your next adventure.

EMILY KIMELMAN
MYSTERIES & THRILLERS

Sydney Rye Mysteries

Unleashed

Death in the Dark

Insatiable

Strings of Glass

Devil's Breath

Inviting Fire

Shadow Harvest

Girl with the Gun

In Sheep's Clothing

Flock of Wolves

Betray the Lie

Savage Grace

Blind Vigilance

Fatal Breach

Undefeated

Relentless

Brutal Mercy

Starstruck Thrillers

A Spy Is Born

EMILY REED

URBAN FANTASY

Kiss Chronicles

Lost Secret

Dark Secret

Stolen Secret

Buried Secret

Date TBA

Lost Wolf Legends

Butterfly Bones

Date TBA

Made in the USA
Columbia, SC
29 July 2024

39565361R00124